CW01660365

RICHARD LEIGH HARRIS was borr
professional musician, lecturer, com
studied at the Birmingham School (
Conservatoire) and Reading Unive
Master of Music degree.

As a writer, Richard has contributed articles and reviews to the following journals: *Avant, Classical Music, Harpsichord & Fortepiano, International Piano, Music Teacher, Musical Opinion Quarterly, The B. S. Johnson Journal, The Musical Times and Tempo.*

Richard was based in Oxford for nearly thirty years, before moving back to Bristol in 2008 where he married in 2010. He is also a qualified reflexologist.

His previous two books, the memoir *The Days of Our Vanity* and the miscellany *My Bermuda Books*, were both published by SilverWood Books in 2012 and 2017, respectively.

He is a member of the British Haiku Society.

By the same author

The Days of Our Vanity (memoir)
My Bermuda Books (miscellany)
Timeslip Fragments (novella)
Bagatelles & Bamboozles (short stories)
Hughie the Hedgehog (for young children)

THE SCALE OF MIDNIGHT AND ELLIPSIS

RICHARD LEIGH HARRIS

To Eva,
happy reading!
Richard x

SilverWood

Published in 2024 by SilverWood Books

SilverWood Books Ltd
14 Small Street, Bristol, BS1 1DE, United Kingdom
www.silverwoodbooks.co.uk

Text copyright © Richard Leigh Harris 2024

The right of Richard Leigh Harris to be identified as the author of this work has been asserted in accordance with the Copyright, Designs and Patents Act 1988 Sections 77 and 78.

All rights reserved. No part of this publication may be reproduced, stored in a retrieval system, or transmitted in any form or by any means, electronic, mechanical, photocopying, recording or otherwise, without prior permission of the copyright holder.

This is a work of fiction. Names, characters, places and incidents either are products of the author's imagination or are used fictitiously. Any resemblance to actual events or locales or persons, living or dead, is entirely coincidental.

ISBN 978-1-80042-267-4 (paperback)

Page design and typesetting by SilverWood Books

This book is dedicated to Helen Hart

Contents

The Scale of Midnight

I had in mind the rare and beautiful tuning I had sometimes heard down by the sea near Sanur… I had already heard this haunting scale at the Javanese court in Bandung. It was the scale of midnight… I had also heard it in Japan, in ancient flute melodies, and at the puppet theatre of Osaka…
(Colin McPhee, *A House in Bali*)

As when a man, about to go forth, prepares a light and kindles a blaze of flaming fire…just so the Fire primeval once lay hid in the round pupil of the eye.
(Empedocles, Greek poet and philosopher)

…don't expect stars in what's coming: nothing will twinkle, this is opaque material… This book is a silence. This book is a question.
(Clarice Lispector, *Hour of the Star*)

1a

Lacunae: absences, gaps, holes, emptinesses – of people, of memory, of consciousness and, therefore, every single thing – and everything.

Extinction and lacunae of individuals, villages and entire cities in countries where democracy is banned. Natural disasters too, of course – that decimate the poorest communities who have the least resources to cope in the aftermath of such events.

+++

1b

In the darkness, the moonlight spreads around the hotel at the edge of the beach, making whiter still those sands which are already dazzlingly white in the daylight sun. But now there are shadows; many-angled shadows.

This beach and its small bay are located on one of the smallest islands off Bali; a very popular destination for holidaymakers and honeymooners alike. On many evenings during the tourist season, the shimmering, interlocking and metallic sounds of a gamelan orchestra echo and resonate around the bay. The majority of visitors think of this as mere entertainment, not realising that this music is both a communal act and a very ancient and sacred tradition.

This island is very beautiful, but is prone to unpredictable weather.

+++

1c

The small village of Little
is no more than a
Historic and notable features of this village include
The church dates from
Notice that

+++

1d

Ian McFlynn, an ophthalmologist of some twenty-five years, is seeing his last patient of the day.

He is meticulous and scrupulous in his work. Likewise his sartorial style, which favours sober suits and spotted or paisley-patterned bow ties. He is tall, slightly stooped, balding, and somewhat overweight around his midriff, and he wears rimless gold spectacles. He speaks quietly, but with a tangible brogue that contains elements of both Irish and Scottish accents. He has been divorced for four years and is prone to sudden flarings of bad temper with the other staff, but virtually never with his patients. He is a man of few words and can seem rather dour on first acquaintance. This initial impression tends to be modified following later meetings. No one doubts his professional abilities, though he does lack a certain charm when dealing with his patients. You could say (and some do) that, in northern parlance, he calls a spade a spade. He would think of this as nothing more than plain speaking, telling things as they are, speaking frankly and to the point. He can also be pedantic, even severe, when something isn't quite right or occurs unexpectedly.

As far as we know, Mr McFlynn has always worked around this area in Hampshire. But you can never tell, can you? For all we know, he might have run wild down under in Australia in his misspent youth. Seen life, been a naughty boy kind of thing. Very unlikely, come to think of it, but you never quite know anyone for certain, do you? Their life, their backstory. Anyone's life, really, come to that. Oh well, he's excellent at his job. Optician? Oh, come on – we all used to be known as opticians when I trained back in the day, some thirty years ago.

+++

1e

I
AM
NOT
SURE
TODAY
REALLY
DEFINES
DIVISION
NECESSITY
ABUNDANTLY
WINDSURFING

'Please read out the letters from the bottom line of the chart.'

'Okay. W-E-M-D-S-O-R-F-E-M-C.'

'Thank you.' McFlynn makes a few notes. 'Now, the fourth word from the bottom, "division". Is it clearer with this...or this? One or two?' He rotated the handle of a mounted lens in his right hand.

'Two, I think.'

'Are you sure?'

'Yes, definitely.'

'Very well, then. We are nearly finished.' A neutral, clipped and precise tone of voice.

Five more minutes and McFlynn had entered the patient's details and measurements into the computer, pronounced himself satisfied, and showed the lady out to the reception desk to pay for her new prescription. Now he sits at his desk and idly taps his pen on the desktop, as though lost in thought. After a few moments, he switches off his computer, his optical equipment, and the lights in his consulting room, puts on his coat and leaves the shop, leaving the receptionist to lock up.

Back at home, he pours himself a large gin and tonic and selects a CD of Beethoven's String Quartet No. 12 in E♭ major, Op. 127. He will prepare himself a small dinner later on. A fastidious eater, he does not care for large meals. After dinner, carefully partnered by a single glass of Bordeaux, he will phone his daughter for their weekly chat. He sips his aperitif slowly, appreciatively, in the same way that he listens to the slow movement of the Beethoven quartet. Unhurried and measured – the way that he does everything, in fact. This is one of his qualities that led to his wife seeking a divorce, and the general perception (on her part, at any rate) of his lack of spontaneity and excitement. He would, if pressed, probably concur with this, in his usual slightly bland demeanour.

+++

1f

'Hello, Dad.'

'Hello, Susie. Good week?'

'Not too bad, thanks. And you?'

It is always like this: curiously formal and stilted.

'Yes, not too bad at all.' He clears his throat, sensing a nervousness in her voice. Then a pause.

'Dad, I'm afraid that I won't be able to come down for Christmas after all,' she blurts out breathlessly. 'You see, we've decided to go to Bali with a couple of friends. Stay over till the New Year.' She grimaces as she says this, feeling guilty and blushing slightly, which, she realises, is rather ridiculous, especially on the phone.

'Oh. That all sounds very exotic, I must say. When was this decided?' A hint of sarcasm there; typical of her father.

'It was a bit on impulse, to be honest. But we thought – well, Colin thought, actually – that it would be a pity to pass up the opportunity. I hope you're not too disappointed?' This last sentence came out more pleadingly than she intended.

Silence.

'Dad?'

'You must do what you feel is appropriate, Susie. Far be it from me to disrupt your travel plans.'

‘What will you do, then? Go to Uncle Michael or Auntie Delia? Or June, maybe?’

‘Probably, yes. To one or the other, I don’t know.’ McFlynn’s heart sinks at the prospect of spending Christmas with either his younger brother in Belfast, or his elder sister and her infinitely dour, whisky-sodden husband on the outskirts of Glasgow. June would definitely be the better option, he thought. Roll on the New Year, everything considered.

A few more desultory comments hung heavily between them before he hung up abruptly, barely saying goodbye. At their respective ends of the phone in County Durham and Hampshire, they both frowned deeply. He felt hurt and betrayed by his only daughter, and she felt guilty, yet angry at his attitude, and with herself for feeling guilty. They had unwittingly (and within mere moments) both entered a state of proud, pig-headed impasse in which neither would willingly give way or concede their position to the other. Unyielding stalemate, basically.

+++

1g

Three weeks later, on the day before Christmas Eve, Susan and Colin flew off on the long-haul flight to Bali from Manchester Airport.

+++

Return to subsection **1b**.

1h

The carol service had been successful; the church almost full. Members of the congregation were now departing after their mince pie and glass of mulled wine, while the churchwarden was checking the pews for any hats, gloves or service sheets. The soprano descants had been inspiring, and it was good to see people there who were not regular worshippers. Perhaps they might be persuaded to attend more often? He also blew out the occasional candle which lazy, forgetful or ignorant members of the congregation had forgotten to snuff out.

'Well done, Ian. Many thanks for your help, as always. Another success, I think?'

'Very much so, Vicar. A lovely service.'

'I'll leave you to lock up, then. See you on Christmas morning.'

'Absolutely.' Ian McFlynn, churchwarden, smiled slowly to himself as the vicar walked rapidly down the aisle and slammed the ancient oak door behind him. McFlynn extinguished the lights and locked the door with the heavy key, then exited the vestry.

+++

Return to **1f** *and/or* **1b**.

2a

The passengers were beginning to settle into the first leg of their long-haul flight, courtesy of Qatar Airways and stopping over at Hamad International Airport in Doha. They were scheduled to land at Ngurah Rai Airport in Denpasar in the early evening of Christmas Eve.

Dinner had been served (a dish of crispy-skinned chicken with ginger, soy, lemongrass, lime, and fragrantly flavoured rice, followed by a raspberry crème brûlée), and the cabin lights had been extinguished. Here and there a passenger read a book or skimmed through a magazine, but the vast majority were dozing after their meal and drinks, including Susan and Colin, her head lolling on his shoulder.

The whole journey, including the stopover, would last approximately eighteen hours and twenty-five minutes.

To the passengers' surprise, the flight landed punctually at Denpasar. A taxi with a very polite and smiling driver was already waiting to transfer Susan and Colin to their beachside hotel. So far, so excellent. Unpack, shower, a drink, then dinner. That would be the agenda for the evening. Perhaps a short walk after dinner, if they were not too tired.

+++

2b

In the darkness, the moonlight spreads and seeps around the corners of the hotel at the edge of the beach. The predominant impression is of whiteness, much whiteness. But there are shadows, deepening shadows…

+++

2c

They held hands as they walked along the beach after dinner. There was a light, warm breeze and the air smelt fresh, almost tangy, which blended in with the woody, cinnamon-fragranced perfume that Susan was wearing.

From inland wafted the exotic, unfamiliar sounds of the gamelan. Low gongs boomed, interjecting; while faster, higher, repeating patterns decorated the lower, slower sounds. It seemed intense and repetitive, yet magical and strange too. An ancient dance and ritual that peeled back the centuries and arrested time. Those stratified layers of percussion. Susan loved the sounds, the subtle weaving of all the parts, while Colin found them merely repetitious and boring.

+++

2d

This island and its region are prone to unpredictable weather.

+++

2e

Christmas Day 2004

Susan and Colin exchanged their presents ('What, no myrrh?' he joked) and ordered a bottle of champagne from room service. For the remainder of the morning they stayed in bed, drinking, making love, dozing, and listening to the regular, gentle swishing of the sea.

In the early afternoon, they stretched sleepily, showered, and ambled down to a late Christmas buffet lunch, enormous and sumptuous in equal measure.

'We won't need to eat for at least a week, darling,' said Susan, nudging Colin in the ribs and giggling as they made their way around the amply laden silver dishes.

Other guests had evidently eaten earlier, as there were plenty of free tables. They chose a table for two as far away from the serenading pianist as possible.

'Well, here's to us, sweetheart: a fantastic Christmas and an equally fantastic New Year. What a country!' said Colin.

They clinked glasses and beamed at each other. The scowling pianist started on yet another hideous carol medley, generously embroidered by rippling arpeggios. Colin sighed, raised his eyebrows and adroitly speared a roast potato, showing it no mercy, imagining it to be the clunky and intrusive pianist.

+++

2f

After the Christmas morning Eucharist, Ian brought over the turkey and two bottles to June's house. A rich, buttery French Chardonnay and a small bottle of dessert wine to accompany the pudding. She had already prepared all the vegetables, he noted approvingly, and built up the fire so that it crackled and spat festively. He hoped that she wouldn't object to him staying overnight, for he wouldn't be in any fit state to drive back home that evening. He would broach that subject later, he decided.

The turkey was drier than he had hoped, but was saved by the quality of the Chardonnay, which, unlike so many brasher New World wines, was not too overtly fruity. June was annoyed about the turkey (apart from the thyme and apricot stuffing), sensing Ian's slight (though unspoken) frisson of displeasure, but the vegetables were tasty and al dente.

They left a gap between the main course and the pudding, deciding to get the majority of the washing-up done and out of the way, thus freeing up time for other pursuits later in the afternoon, such as a game of chess. They both hated to lose and were apt to sulk, although June was the slightly better and more strategic player, being able to think ahead laterally by several moves.

She beat Ian at chess but, as a form of compensation, let him stay over. In certain ways, she was well aware that she was the queen (cunning and variable in her possible moves and potential attacks), while he was, unknowingly, a mere pawn in her long-term game plan.

+++

2g

After a small, late supper (rice and crab meat served on a banana leaf, plus ice-cold beers), and in an attempt to escape the boisterousness of the hotel's entertainment activities, Susan and Colin walked down to the beach. It was just after 11pm and neither of them felt like sleeping. They sat in silence for some minutes, enjoying the quiet. Time didn't really seem to matter any more. It had been a virtually perfect Christmas Day, apart from the restaurant pianist.

The next morning, they took another stroll on the beach before breakfast.

'That's odd,' said Colin, peering intently out into the bay.

'What is?'

'Well, I might be imagining it, but the sea seems to have receded. Have a look.'

Susan followed his gaze. 'I haven't got my lenses in,' she said, squinting in the direction in which he was now pointing.

For a moment he stood absolutely still. A vein in his right temple started to throb. 'Listen.'

'I can't hear anything.'

'Precisely. Where's the sound of the sea, the surf on the beach? The sea just out beyond the bay and the reef has *definitely* receded. We must go. *Right now*,' he said brusquely and urgently, between gulps of air. He checked his watch. It was 7.57am local time; 11.57pm GMT.

'But, Colin, I want to swim...' she began to protest.

'No time.' He grabbed her by the hand and started to drag her back towards the hotel.

'You're hurting my arm, let go!' she shrilled, glaring at him.

'Run, Susan. *Run!*' he shouted, letting go of her hand and sprinting away.

He was ahead of her. She cried out. He glanced back. She had tripped and fallen, stubbed her toe on a rock, twisted her ankle or something, the stupid girl. It was enough to make a difference; all the difference. But against his better instincts, something was telling him that he could not, dare not turn back for her. As he ran, the sounds of the gamelan pounded in his ears, fiercer, faster and louder, together with a roaring behind him from the beach, as if emitted by some terrible primeval creature.

+++

2h

The small village of Little Tockington lies some six miles east of Brockenhurst in Hampshire and is little more than a hamlet of ancient cottages. It is mentioned, briefly, in the Domesday Book. Historic and notable features of this village include the Church of St Boniface, the oldest parts of which date back to the mid-thirteenth century. Walk on past the church, and within two hundred yards the visitor will come upon the only public house in the village, The Olde Bull, which dates back to the sixteenth century. Note that some of the original timber beams are still in place. Just past the pub is a covered well, used until the late nineteenth century – its waters were rumoured to be restorative, and subsequently it was venerated as a holy well. There is also an abandoned watermill nearby…

…stated the anonymous author of the guidebook to the village.

+++

Return to **2d** *and/or* **2c**.

2i

Susan lay there, not moving. Her body was covered by debris and mud.

Colin had nearly made it back to the hotel, but one of the walls surrounding the hotel garden had collapsed on him, trapping and crushing his legs. He was found some hours later.

They had both died with the sound of the gamelan playing the scale of midnight ringing and echoing in their ears, together with the crescendoing roar of the tsunami as it made landfall, pulverising anything and everything in its path.

+++

2j

Ian McFlynn sat bolt upright in bed. 'Oh God, oh God!'

'What's the matter, darling?' June turned towards him. She clicked on the bedside light and glanced at the clock. It was 2.10am. His face was almost ashen and there was a panicked look in his eyes. She hugged him to her, cradling him in her arms; his pyjama top was soaked with sweat and his body felt taut and tense.

'I've just dreamed of Susan, my daughter Susan. She was… she was on a beach and she was smiling and waving at me, saying something about "Everything's going to be all right." But I'm sure that she's dead. I just know it: I feel it in my bones that she's gone.' He was trembling now, and very hot.

'You've had a bad dream, that's all. Sit up and I'll make us a cup of tea, okay?'

He nodded weakly, as June rearranged his pillows and then padded downstairs barefoot. He heard her filling the kettle, the click of the switch being depressed, and then the faint sound of milk splashing into cups. It was going to be a long night.

They sipped their tea and talked.

3am. He felt refreshed by the tea and had washed his face and neck in cold water. His whole body had cooled down and he was much calmer now. They kissed, then drifted off into a light sleep.

At the end of the day, Lord, keep us and bless us.

+++

3a

Survivors talked of a roaring, massive wall of water, coming in groups of two or three onslaughts, as if each mighty wave gathered, then expelled, a huge surge of energy. A tsunami, in other words. The scale of midnight. The scale of devastation. Beachside hotels had been swept away, vanished in the blink of an eye; a massive aqueous eye.

The epicentre was off the west coast of Sumatra, with a magnitude on the Richter scale of 9.1 to 9.3. This was an undersea megathrust earthquake that caused a rupture along the fault between the Burma Plate and the India Plate. The tsunami made landfall at 7.58am on Boxing Day. The first signs of abnormal conditions were the receding ocean and the frothing bubbles on its surface. The incoming waves were measured at between fifty and one hundred feet high (fifteen to thirty metres), and the eventual death toll over fourteen countries was estimated to be around 227,898 people, with many thousands more surviving (some injured) and being displaced due to the destruction of their homes.

Furious, futile and inane destruction. Everything in its wake, from fishing boats to shops and hotels. Cars inverted, upended on roofs; a moving river of bodies and bricks flowing inland until it was halted by a wall of piled-up debris, against which the waters backed up, trying to escape. Too late for that.

Oh
no,
God!
Jesus!
Merciful
centrifugally

+++

3b

Rupture.

Latent phenomenon.

Cataclysmic, catastrophic perdition.

Usurping terror of underwater chasms.

Massive breaking up of huge…and unsuspected zawns.

A far larger, more aqueous…Aberfan, but still with sucking, slurping black oozings.

An overwhelming blackness from the depths, devouring the other, upper darkness of night and obliterating the stars of the heavens.

Vast and deep-lying tectonic plates shifted unexpectedly to rub roughly against one another, setting up huge seismic collisions and explosions never dreamed of by humans who were not sufficiently aware of these eruptions.

+++

3c

Then another wave hit the island: that of the radio microphones and television journalists. Sympathetic in their own way and letting the wider world know what had happened, thus ensuring that aid and money flowed in during the following weeks (until another, larger crisis hit the headlines), but still managing to get in the way of the rescue and clear-up operation.

Various agencies then became involved, including the International Committee of the Red Cross, Médecins Sans Frontières and other helpers. Local resources, including rescue workers with drilling equipment, worked tirelessly, but were hampered by the physical devastation and the limitations or lack of local infrastructures.

The body count was rising inexorably, and now there was the added risk of waterborne diseases. Some miles inland, the hospital had survived intact and was doing what it could to cope with the injured and the dying, though the stock of analgesics was running low and the power supply was very sporadic.

+++

3d

From among the English tourists holidaying on the island, two bodies have been identified from dental records. They are Susan McFlynn, 25, and a man believed to be her partner, Colin Croshaw, 28, both teachers of English as a foreign language from County Durham.

+++

3e

The men were mostly silent, standing rooted to the spot, or were wandering around in small circles, just pacing, dazed and robotic, gesticulating wildly yet forlornly over the loss of their family members and houses. Or they scrabbled frantically through the debris to find something, anything, from their vanished homes, making small moaning sounds as they did so.

Women and their wide-eyed children were openly weeping or wailing loudly, some on the verge of screaming; looking to heaven or back towards the terrible sea, shaking their fists at a cruel and merciless God.

'Where is my son? Where is my son?' shouted a young mother, over and over; a frantic mantra.

'We are looking, my love. We are looking, I promise you,' said an aid worker, putting her arm around the inconsolable woman, who was rocking back and forth, as if cradling an invisible child.

+++

3f

Five hours later.

'Here is your son.'

The aid worker passed the toddler gently into the arms of his mother. The boy's hair was matted with dust and mud, but he was breathing and looking blearily up into his mother's eyes. She cradled him to her breast and tears began to run down both cheeks.

'Bless you, bless you. It is a miracle. Thank you, thank you.' She shook her head in disbelief. Then, almost as a whispered afterthought, 'And my daughter?'

'We will keep searching,' said the aid worker, opening her arms wide in what she thought would be interpreted as a gesture of hope.

The mother nodded and clung to her son, smiling slightly. 'I will pray.'

The aid worker nodded at her, but without any real conviction. She walked away, hoping against doubtful hope. This was, after all, just one desperate mother among so many.

+++

3g

Ian McFlynn took the call, but he had already read the papers and watched the television bulletins. The speaker's tone at the other end of the line sounded apologetic, but also grave and subdued, as if he were used to being the bearer of bad news. McFlynn replaced the receiver and stared blankly at it. The man had sounded absolutely certain of his daughter's identity. He *knew* that she shouldn't have gone on holiday with that new boyfriend of hers; had been certain that something awful would happen. Outside, the light was fading and the rain was lashing down, seeming to mirror McFlynn's copious tears. It would have been a miracle had she survived, he thought, pulling the curtains. But miracles do not happen in this life, however much one may wish for them, he reflected.

+++

3h

It was a surreal, unimaginable landscape. While entire buildings had been crushed, smaller artefacts such as mopeds had been left standing upright, seemingly with no damage. Electric cookers lay abandoned on their sides, while metal gongs and smaller gamelan instruments glinted in the emerging sunlight, upturned in mud and covered in branches. Some larger trees remained virtually intact, but not many. This day, both humanity and hope lay in ruined tatters, at least in this region of the planet.

+++

3i

The aid workers had to break the news to the mother that they had been unable to locate her daughter. When the waters receded, the girl's body would be discovered. Meanwhile, the mother silently rocked her son to and fro, to and fro, to and fro, as if in a repetitive trance. For, after this calamity, what else did she have? What else could she do but revert to her gut-and-heart instinct to be a protective mother? To cling on to the only thing that she possessed?

+++

I had thought of culling reports of this tsunami from various newspapers such as *The Times*, *The Guardian*, *The Telegraph*, et cetera. But we can imagine those reports for ourselves, can't we? The nature and the content of them. The micro and macro levels of devastation, the accounts of bodies laid out, the vast swathes of structural damage, and the almost unimaginable state of pandemonium. There would also be the thorny and possibly protracted issue of copyright permissions.

That penultimate sentence reminds me of a joke – and there are not too many of them (if any) in this book, so perhaps this will lighten the mood temporarily (at roughly the midpoint of this novella), given the sheer darkness of the circumstances. This is it.

A pandamonium is similar to a harmonium, except that it requires two pandas to play it: one to play the keyboard; the other to pump the pedals (the latter being particularly necessary if the keyboard-playing panda is rather small). Not forgetting a plentiful supply of bamboo shoots to keep them both happy and to sustain their energy, of course.

Looking back, the media *in toto* seemed to display a barely concealed, ghoulish pleasure in the tsunami tragedy that was, to say the least, distasteful and thoroughly inappropriate.

3j

A light was on in the Church of St Boniface, Little Tockington. It was nearly midnight.

The vicar was returning from walking his dog when he noticed it. He took the dog home, patted it and whispered a few words in its ear, closed the front door of the vicarage, and headed down the path to the church, whose normally sharp outlines were blurred by an increasingly thick mist. He shut the door quietly and let his eyes adjust to the gloom. The chancel light revealed a man in shadow kneeling at the altar rail, cursing and weeping and smiting the rail with his right fist. He was evidently in much distress. The vicar tiptoed up to where he knelt and saw that the man's profile and head shape were familiar, though hunched and stooped.

'Ian. What has happened?'

The tear-stained, reddened face of Ian McFlynn, ophthalmologist and churchwarden, looked up. 'Vicar. Will you please stay and pray with me for a few minutes? Please?' His voice was tremulous, urgent.

'Of course. What's wrong?'

'It's Susan. She's been killed. Killed in the tsunami. Her boyfriend Colin was also killed.' Ian spoke raspingly in between gasps of breath; then he reached for a handkerchief and dabbed at his eyes.

The vicar's arm cradled his shoulder to comfort him. For a few moments he held him without speaking. 'Shall we pray?'

Ian nodded.

'Lord, strengthen Your servant Ian at this terrible time of the loss of his daughter and her partner and all those who have been killed in the Indonesian tsunami. We also pray for and remember their families at this time of tragedy. May Ian truly know and sense Your love and be embraced by the power of Your all-encompassing, never-failing light. We humbly ask that the soul of Susan dwell forever in the circle of Your nearer presence, Lord. Amen.'

'Amen.'

'I suggest that we now recite the night hymn, "*Te Lucis Ante Terminum*". Is that all right?'

Ian nodded his assent. They knelt together, shoulders touching, as the vicar spoke gently and reassuringly, but firmly.

To Thee before the close of day,
Creator of the world, we pray
That, with Thy wonted favour, Thou
Wouldst be our guard and keeper now.
From all ill dreams defend our sight,
From fears and terrors of the night;
Withhold from us our ghostly foe,
That spot of sin we may not know.
O Father, that we ask be done,
Through Jesus Christ, Thine only Son,
Who, with the Holy Ghost and Thee,
Doth live and reign eternally.

They remained silent for a minute or two; then the vicar helped McFlynn to his feet and guided him down the aisle, out of the church and to his car. They shook hands.

'Phone me at any time if you need anything.'

McFlynn nodded his thanks and opened his car door, but didn't make to sit down in the driving seat. He just stood rooted to the spot, unable or unwilling to move. The vicar disappeared into the swirling mist, as if he had been an apparition.

A holy ghost, indeed.

+++

3k

She spotted him standing alone on the bonnet of a car. He was small and was holding out his arms, as if in search of his mother – or any mother. He appeared both exhausted and fearful, sometimes turning his head to survey the wreckage that stretched to the horizon. She picked her way gingerly over the debris and waved at him as she approached.

'Don't be afraid.' She offered her hand, then gave him a hug. 'I'm Bethari,[1] who are you?'

'Raharjo.'[2]

'Hello, Raharjo,' said Bethari, smiling and taking his hand in hers. They stood and surveyed the acres of rice fields, many of which were flooded. 'I'm eight. How old are you?'

'Six, I think.' A long pause. 'Can I ask you something?'

'Of course.'

'Are you an orphan?'

'I can't find my parents, so probably yes.'

'Oh. So that's what "orphan" means.'

'Yes, it does. Sorry.'

---

1 Javanese form of Batari; the name of a goddess.

2 Plentiful; abundant.

'Me too.' His eyes widened in alarm and he suddenly began to cry large, copious, plopping tears which fell onto his trainers.

'Try not to worry, Raharjo. I'll take care of you. After all, we're both in the same boat, aren't we?'

He nodded, wiping his nose on his sleeve. 'My dad was in a fishing boat when this happened,' he said, gesturing around an invisible bay with his right index finger.

'We were sleeping and then the house cracked in two. I think my parents either escaped or were buried.' She grimaced. 'I tried to look for them, but it was too dangerous.'

'What caused it?'

'Something to do with the sea. It sort of boiled over.'

He looked puzzled, frowning slightly, but didn't ask her any more questions.

'What we need to do now,' she said, bending down and looking him straight in the face, 'is find food and shelter, okay? Shall we do that?'

He nodded rapidly several times.

'The big school near the hospital in the middle of the island is being used to help all the people like us. I heard someone talking about it earlier. It's only about seven miles and we can walk there in a couple of hours. The grown-ups can help us find our parents.'

They stood still for a moment, then Bethari took Raharjo's hand in hers and they began to walk purposefully inland, along the debris-strewn road, where barely any buildings had survived. She exclaimed at the ferocity of the damage, pointing out wrecked vehicles, but he didn't really want to see.

'Makes me sad,' he said, staring straight ahead and putting one hand to the side of his face, trying to blot out the devastation.

'Yes, me too,' she replied, squeezing his other hand as they trudged their way towards the centre of the island.

After half an hour's walking, the landscape still looked as if a bomb had decimated it.

'I'm a bit hungry,' he said suddenly, pulling on her hand like an eager puppy on a leash.

'We'll find some food soon, when we get to the school,' she said, with more confidence than she was actually feeling. 'Come on, we have to keep going. We can do this.'

Looking for all the world like a little brother and big sister, the two figures receded into the distance. A long camera shot, as if at the end of a film; the lead couple walking into the sunset or some other cliché, but more godforsaken.

Re. sea: dead. Reseeded.

+++

31

At the school in the middle of the island, Father Egan O'Flaherty was helping to distribute comfort and bowls of rice to the many homeless. A much-loved priest, he had grown up just outside Skibbereen in County Cork. Known to many of his parishioners back home as 'Angel' (an anagrammatic conflation of his Christian name and the 'l' from his surname) on account of his pastoral empathy and devotion to his flock, he had felt the call of his ministry to move overseas and serve the island community here in Indonesia. At least, that was the official version of the story circulated by his local bishop back in south-east Ireland.

At more or less the same moment, give or take a few seconds, that Father O'Flaherty was reciting '*Te Lucis Ante Terminum*' with a group of the homeless, the vicar of St Boniface in Little Tockington, Hampshire, thousands of miles across the globe, was sharing the same hymn with Ian McFlynn at the altar rail.

Give or take, yes. The taking away of lives, innocent or otherwise. God's method of controlling the spiralling population? Possibly, and in a few terrible seconds, too.

The Lord giveth and He taketh away…

Synchronicity. What are the chances of that? Or, to be more precise, what is the statistical probability of this occurring? A random coincidence, or all part of a calculated, divine plan? Heads or tails? Or two people with the same first name being murdered at precisely the same moment, hundreds of miles apart, for example. I'm not a mathematician, nor a seer, so if you want some light cast on this subject, I suggest that you look it up for yourselves. Okay?

+++

Return to **3h**.

3m

'I'm still hungry,' complained Raharjo, 'and thirsty.' His head was down and his body language was a mixture of tiredness and sulkiness.

'The same here,' responded Bethari, 'but don't drink the water: it will give you a bad stomach. Wait until we get to the centre.'

'Okay.'

They trudged on in silence, Raharjo occasionally kicking at a stone or a branch.

'Not much further – we're nearly there,' said Bethari. 'Look, we're on the outskirts of the town already.' She pointed.

Their steps began to quicken.

+++

3n

One of Father O'Flaherty's volunteers greeted Bethari and Raharjo as they wandered into the refugee centre. 'Sit down. You must be hungry.'

They nodded in unison. The woman ushered them to two chairs and a rickety table and brought them two bowls of rice. They ate quickly with their hands and were then given a bottle of lukewarm Coke each.

'Now, we need a few details,' said the same lady, armed with a pen and clipboard. 'Brother and sister?' she enquired, smiling.

'No, just new friends,' said Bethari. 'I found him on top of a car and he looked lost.'

'Of course,' said the lady sympathetically.

'We want you to find our parents, please. If that's possible,' said Bethari, playing with her hair.

'We will do our best for you,' the woman replied. She smiled, but then suddenly turned her face from them and moved away.

Raharjo's eyes panned around the hall, a slow camera, absorbing the misery of the people. He began to weep again.

They sat down on the floor and were given two blankets. Huddled next to them and barely uttering a word were a father and son, embraced in and by sorrow, bent towards one another in shared grief.

Picasso could well have painted them in his Blue Period. Bethari nudged Raharjo, gesturing with her head, but put her forefinger to her lips, cautioning him to say nothing.

Indeed, nothing was exactly what they had: the shared coin; the common denominator in this catastrophe that rendered normally voluble people mute. As if language had deserted them; was unable to find the requisite, appropriate words for this situation in the aftermath of seemingly random devastation and destruction.

Bethari and Raharjo laid down their heads on the thin blankets and tried to get to sleep, in spite of the assorted groanings and moanings coming from various parts of the hall.

There were no pillows.

+++

30

Three days after the tsunami, Bethari stepped outside into the early morning air, stretched and yawned. Without knowing why, she suddenly looked up at the sky. High above her, approaching slowly, was a solitary eagle. The bird was majestic, its head glancing from side to side as it glided on the thermals. Bethari shaded her eyes and watched. This was, she realised (based on memories of her school lessons), the legendary Garuda, the national symbol of Indonesia and a lucky talisman to behold. The bird dropped gracefully, dipped leisurely lower, seeming to hover so that the girl could get a better view. For a few moments, Bethari could have vouched on her parents' lives that the eagle was looking directly at her, almost piercingly *through* her, as if it were aware of her predicament. Perhaps this is a sign of hope for us all? she thought.

She ran back into the school to summon a still-sleepy Raharjo, beckoning urgently. 'Quickly! Quickly! Come and see the huge eagle!'

He rubbed his eyes and stumbled out after her, but by the time they had run outside, the bird had vanished, as if it had never been, or as if it had been a mere figment of the girl's imagination.

Raharjo said nothing, but gave Bethari a withering look that spoke volumes. 'I want my breakfast,' he said sulkily, turning away from her and walking determinedly indoors, his head hanging in disappointment and disbelief that his new friend and (almost) sister had lied to him.

+++

Return to **3b**.

4a

McFlynn took two weeks off work to sort out his daughter's funeral, make various calls to the appropriate embassy in London, and drive north to clear Susan's flat in County Durham. There was so much paperwork to complete and numerous demands were being made by the various authorities involved; all, of course, at the very time when he felt least able to cope with the mental pressure and the physical exhaustion. Sorting through Susan's clothes and possessions was the worst of all of his tasks. His walk slowed to a geriatric-like crawl, and at each step he felt as if he were wading through treacle; attempting to escape some endless quagmire not of his own making. He also informed his ex-wife by writing her a short and tersely worded letter that, in hindsight, even he admitted could have been more sympathetic.

After the two weeks he resumed work, but found it almost impossible to concentrate. Ironically, the stress and anxiety affected his vision, making objects appear remote and clouded, as was his professional judgement. June, also an ophthalmologist in the same shop, suggested that he needed more time to recuperate, and reluctantly he heeded her advice. Temporarily (and on her insistence), he moved into her house so that she could keep an eye on him, as his behaviour seemed to be becoming somewhat erratic.

The funeral approached slowly and heavily, came and went, and was terrible in its intense outpouring of grief. But now it was done, over with, and he had somehow (though he knew not how) got through it without collapsing in a crumpled heap, either literally or metaphorically. More worrying to his unsettled mind was the fact that he could recall so little of Susan's life, beyond the Kodak photos that he still possessed of her as a child; a girl transforming into a slightly stroppy (though by no means impossible) teenager. It was as if grief had erased his memory; as if he were staring into a huge, stagnant pool of amnesia.

+++

Return to **3d**, *then* **3g** *and* **2j**.

4b

They discussed the possibility of grief affecting the functioning of the eyes; particularly the ability to focus. Ian agreed that his eyes were behaving oddly and unpredictably. Was this malfunctioning of his eyes affecting his mind, or was his mind affecting his eyes? It was impossible to know, but he felt that there was a definite correlation between the two. This led to an observation by June that some of the greatest writers had been blind, including Milton, Borges and Joyce. Somewhat shamefully, they both admitted that neither of them had read anything by those three authors.

'Probably a good idea to start with Borges,' Ian suggested. 'At least his fictions are short.'

They agreed that this wasn't the time to attempt Joyce's *Ulysses*. You had to be feeling strong for that one; oh yes, indeed. There was no arguing with that.

June went on the internet and looked up other writers who had been blind. According to this particular search engine, they included Galileo Galilei, Homer, Helen Keller, Wyndham Lewis, James Thurber, Paul Groussac and José Mármol, the last two of whom neither June nor Ian had heard of. Remarkably few, then, given the sheer number of writers over the centuries. Next time I'll look up blind composers and painters. If I take the time, I could assemble a whole cornucopian list of creative blindness! June thought, pondering on the prospect with an increasingly wide grin. Then she could attempt a list of all those creators who were afflicted by deafness; chief of whom, of course, was Beethoven.

+++

4c

The idea came to him, suddenly, while he was out for a walk. He knew that it was beyond the pale; was not what one was supposed to do; was insane, mad, nuts, bonkers, even – all of those words and more still. But the time for merely rational armchair contemplation of the various possibilities had come and passed. It was now time for action; and now, he had that time. The important thing was to come up with a watertight plan and to ensure that there were no mistakes. Yes, an operation; that was what was required. The thought of all of this made him breathe faster and feel hot. No, he couldn't do this alone. He must get help, but from where and from whom? Yes, it was time to make the necessary plans and get going. The opportunity lay in front of him, even if certain sacrifices would have to be made. No time like the present. The time for action was now, most definitely. His steps quickened towards home and he had a glint in his eye.

+++

4d

The body was discovered in mid-March, in the morning following a light dusting of overnight snow, just inside the west-facing wall of the churchyard of St Boniface at Little Tockington.

The young woman lay face down behind one of the gravestones, the snow on the back of her head resembling wedding confetti. There had been no attempt by the perpetrator to cover, let alone bury, her body. Her left arm lay close to her side, while her head rested in the crook of her right arm, facing upwards and to the left, her right cheek on the ground. Her lipstick and mascara were still intact.

It was established that she was in her mid-twenties. The pathologist opined that her death would have been quick and that she would have barely felt a thing. She had not been raped or interfered with, gagged or bound; but had been struck from behind with a heavy (possibly blunt) object. Surprisingly, there was little in the way of bruising evident behind the hairline, although a small amount of blood had seeped from her right ear, pooled and congealed. Apart from a couple of streaks of mud, her face was white as marble, but looked peaceful.

+++

Return to **2j**.

4e

Bethari and Raharjo were still being cared for in the school-cum-community centre. Clothes, food, drink and occasional classes were given, and various games organised for both the adults and the children. Wherever appropriate, the abler and fitter adults were asked to help in supervising the children. Among them were three teachers. Bethari and Raharjo cried less frequently now, and overnight Bethari had virtually become a mother to the boy, looking out for him in every possible way. In the aftermath of the tsunami, they had had to grow up very quickly.

Five weeks after the disaster, the authorities found a couple in their late thirties who were not only willing to foster both of the children, but genuinely delighted and excited at the prospect of doing so. Within days, and once the necessary paperwork and documentation were in order, Bethari and Raharjo began their new life with their new parents on the other side of the island. The children were adored by the couple and, in their turn and over time, grew to trust and love them. Most of all, they felt safe and secure in their new home. Routines were established and boundaries set, and the quartet lived harmoniously together, each pair reflecting periodically on how lucky they were to have found each other. Bethari often thought of the eagle that she had seen that day; seemingly aloof but somehow caring too, in a way that she still found puzzling and couldn't fathom.

+++

Return to **3h**.

4f

Ian and June were having dinner in The Olde Bull. Amid the clinking of cutlery, most of the conversations centred around the recent murder. It was virtually the sole topic of conversation, be it at the bar or in the restaurant. Ian and June looked at each other, raised their eyebrows and grimaced, before starting on their scallops with curry oil, sultanas and shavings of apple. Accompanying this was a well-chilled bottle of New Zealand Sauvignon Blanc, full of heady gooseberry and lime. They raised their glasses to one another.

'Slainte.'

'Slainte.'

They clinked glasses.

'Must be some local bastard,' commented a red-faced man loudly to his wife. They were sitting at an adjacent table. 'Local knowledge and all that.' He nodded sagely in a self-satisfied manner.

His wife merely nodded and glanced away, as if she had heard it all before.

'If he is local, we'll get him all right, don't you worry. Send the lads round, teach him a lesson he'll never forget and all that malarkey.'

'I won't worry. And, just for the record, it might not be a he, for all you know,' added his tight-lipped wife.

The husband paused, mid-steak, lay down his knife and fork and just looked at her. 'Pass the pepper, will you?' was all he said, but with an unmistakable edge to his voice.

'Marriage, eh?' whispered Ian to June from behind his hand.

June winked back, saying nothing, but thinking quite a lot.

They were too full to make love, so contented themselves with a game of chess over a glass or two of port. Within a few tactically devastating moves, June took Ian's queen and thus commenced a total annihilation of his army. Too tired to be angry or humiliated, he merely shook his head and laughed. He was beginning to get used to this.

+++

4g

Okay, okay. Stay calm and don't run. Don't run, whatever you do. Go to work as normal, plan ahead, be methodical and keep up appearances. Don't get ahead of yourself. Any slip-ups could prove costly. Everything could turn inside out and upside down. Be very careful.

You're never going to be off duty now, not even for the smallest of moments. You'll have to keep glancing over your shoulder. Can you live with that? Are you certain? It's your choice; or, rather, if you pursue this path, you will have no choice; zero choice at all. Your decision.

+++

4h

The beach appeared endless. A cloudless cerulean-blue sky, also without beginning or end; the two vastnesses of beach and sky merging effortlessly into one another, for mile upon mile.

In the far distance, a girl emerged from the sea, towelling her hair vigorously. She ran up the beach towards him, but in exaggerated, filmic slow motion, and she was beaming and laughing, joyous and carefree. Of course – how could it be otherwise? The figure was Susan, his dead daughter, smiling and waving at him as she used to, with that way of tilting her head, almost cheekily, to one side (her right side). Waving at him, merrily, but with a sense of urgency, of a 'Come on, you must come with me now' kind, urging him to join her. But he held his ground, could not move, would not join her, as much as part of him desperately wanted to; indeed, wanted nothing more. After a few moments of holding his gaze, she pointed to the sky, then turned her back and slowly, deliberately walked back into the sea without glancing back.

Oh Jesus, sweet Jesus, was all that he could think, shaking his head several times, as if to dismiss that overwhelmingly strong, lifelike image of her. No matter how hard he tried, the image would not go; would not let him go; buried itself in and clung to all the crevices and recesses of his mind.

He wasn't dreaming, but neither was he awake; more suspended between two not wholly defined worlds or states of being. Dawn light seeped through the curtains. June was sleeping soundly beside him, making soft but deep and throaty purring noises. He lay motionless, his eyes closed and his hands on his chest, as though in prayer or rehearsing for death; the way he would be lain out in his coffin. His mind was racing and turning, racing and turning.

+++

4i

They drove into the nearest town, parked up and headed for the smallish but sufficiently ample branch of Waterstones. Initially he had been reluctant, but she had persuaded him with the promise of lunch at a local bistro. Even so, he was grumbling under his breath about being almost blinded by the sheer number of damn books in the shop; the too-huge amount of choice. Choice, he decided, was often an overrated attribute.

'Well, what else would you *expect* from a bookshop?' She shot him a glance, sounding slightly miffed.

'Fair point.'

She had entered with the intention of browsing randomly, but almost immediately (and serendipitously?) put her hand on the sole remaining copy of Clarice Lispector's *Hour of the Star*. He was still dithering, so she went to pay for her Penguin Modern Classic, while he sat in a deep chair that almost engulfed him.

She strode back to him. 'Found anything?' Her tone was more conciliatory.

'Yes. I think I'll have this.' He waved the cover in her face. It was an anthology of haiku, from Matsuo Basho, the acknowledged master of the form, through to more recent and somewhat mangled offerings.

Ohsab, she thought to herself, reversing Basho's name. It could almost be Japanese, particularly if the 'h' was omitted.

'Don't think I can face anything much more demanding,' he said, almost apologetically.

'Hmm. 365 – one for each day of the year. That should keep you occupied,' she said.

Did he detect a soupçon of sarcasm? If he did, he let it go.

'Let's get that lunch,' he said. 'All these bloody books drain the air, suck up the oxygen and make you hungry.'

'You're always hungry,' she said, elbowing him in what he took to be an affectionate gesture.

'Fast metabolism,' he responded, grinning slightly and shrugging his shoulders.

They hastened towards the bistro.

+++

Return to **1e**.

4j

Father O'Flaherty stopped his slow pacing, adjusted his dog collar, then put his hands in his pockets, looked directly at the children over the top of his half-glasses, and cleared his throat. 'Today, we're all going to learn a new word. It is a very special word, a traditional Javanese word. It is "*iklas*": it is spelled I-K-L-A-S, okay? Say the word with me. *Iklas*, that's right. It sounds and *is* a beautiful word, and it means a state of mind that has no emotion troubling it. No anger, no sadness or happiness. That seems quite odd, doesn't it?'

He glanced around at the children, some of whom nodded vigorously, including Bethari.

O'Flaherty continued. 'To us, that might seem impossible. Like when we find our sums and maths problems very hard, yes?' He smiled a wide, beaming, inclusive smile, over and into the large group of children sat at his feet. 'Well, yes, it *is* hard. But over many, many years – hundreds and thousands of years, in fact – some very holy and special men and women have managed to achieve this state of peace. How did they manage it? After many hours of devotion, practice and prayer, they became so quiet and peaceful that they were aware only of their own breath and their slow heartbeat. Emotions no longer mattered to them. That's amazing, isn't it?'

More nods of general consent and approval, if not of understanding.

'A good way of remembering the word "*iklas*" is to think of it like this. "I" is for "I", "K" is for "know", "L" is for "large", "A" is for "amazing" and "S" is for "sun". *I know large, amazing sun.*' He gestured for them all to join him in saying the sentence. 'That's called a mnemonic, which you don't need to know about, but we all know about the sun, don't we? It's what powers our earth and gives us all life.' Even if it is excruciatingly bloody hot, he thought to himself, mopping his profusely sweating forehead. 'I think that that's enough for now, children. Go off and get a drink and I'll see you tomorrow. And don't forget that beautiful word now, will you?' He wagged a mock-admonishing finger at them, accompanied by a slight wink from his left eye.

Then Father Egan O'Flaherty, son of Skibbereen, strode off in search of a drink which, in all probability, was not going to be orange squash. In fact, come to think of it, you could have put a bet on it. Indeed, as he had said himself on numerous occasions after Mass, 'and for the adults, there will be drink'.

+++

5a

The gaping lacuna of her absence was palpable and terrible. Susan was in his head both day and night, whether he wanted her there or not. Between the hazy grey states of sleeping and waking, her face was suspended within a ball of light, seemingly located only at the end of the bed, yet nonetheless out of reach. Her body was not visible. She was no longer on the beach (which had vanished), and her expression was now unsmiling, staring sternly, and unchanging. Accusatory; that was how Ian McFlynn saw it. He very slowly opened his left eye a fraction and followed, from left to right, the floating blue-black creatures; the tadpole lines on his retina; the delicate film of greyish lace moving in its languorous swayings. He let these almost comforting patterns pass over to the right eye, then back and forth a few times, without haste.

Beside him, June was slowly emerging into wakefulness, yawning and stretching. Time for tea. He glanced involuntarily towards the end of the bed, but Susan's face was not there now and he felt relieved. Leadenly, he walked the few steps to the en suite bathroom. A pee before the tea would be advisable.

+++

5b

It was during the last week of May that one of the parishioners of St Boniface discovered the second body.

Again, it was a young female and the same modus operandi seemed to have been employed: i.e. that of being hit on the head from behind, leaving the victim with no chance of seeing her assailant. A cowardly assault, in other words. Once more, the young lady had not been raped or sexually interfered with in any way, and looked peaceful in repose.

The local police were rather more proactive and diligent on this occasion, setting up house-to-house enquiries and urging all the local men to drop in at the station for DNA testing.

+++

5c

Opaque material, this, you might think. Yes, you – the reader.

It was June's day off. After lunch, and with her feet tucked up underneath her on the sofa, she took a lengthy sip of a Venetian Pinot Grigio that she had begun with her salad. She turned the page of Clarice Lispector's *Hour of the Star*. Her eyes skimmed the page. Almost immediately she read the words 'nothing will twinkle, this is opaque material'. She looked up at the sun illuminating specks of dust which rotated lazily in the air in front of her. Lispector's slim book dropped from her hand and she sank into a short doze.

Nothing will twinkle…

+++

5d

The body of the third young woman was discovered at the end of the last week of June.

Once more, the perpetrator had attacked her from behind, and her body lay, or had been placed, alongside the wall of St Boniface's churchyard.

This victim displayed one important difference, however. Her right eye had been gouged from its socket and removed; perhaps kept by the killer as a gruesome souvenir.

+++

5e

I'll hold on, hold off for as long as possible, if not longer. Whatever that means. What does anything mean now, for Christ's sake? Imperative to go. Tell them that I've had a relapse; need some more time off, yes. Plenty of staff, after all. Book the ferry, drive diagonally across the middle of Ireland and stay out of sight; keep my head down in some backwater off the coast in Clare. Contact Sean, perhaps?

Is that a plan? Is it good enough, foolproof? Yes, it's a good plan. Watertight, as far as I can see. How far ahead do I need to see? For how long? A day at a time is ample for now. I'll book the early afternoon crossing for two days' time. Slowly but surely wins the day. Is that a mixed metaphor? Who cares? Best to start packing, but not too large a bag. Draw attention. Might be police at Fishguard. Say I'm attending a conference, if questioned. Better not refuse a DNA swab either, if I'm stopped. Lucky to have avoided it up until now. Okay, boy, think straight, keep your mind clear and don't get distracted. If things get tricky, then as a last resort I'll drown myself. But where? At some godforsaken resort? No – better done and got over with in a narrow, nondescript and not-too-deep river. Ha! Better for whom, eh? Certainly not me. But for her? No, it won't ever come to that, you idiot. Well, that's not wrong, to be sure, is it? I'm certainly an idiot, and a huge one at that. A vast eejit, in fact.

There's no denying it. But a sure thing? Now then, that's a different matter again.

+++

5f

'God have mercy on your soul and your myriad wickedness.'

Susan watched her father, as did his parents and the souls of the three victims, and, of course, God Himself. A sevenfold accusation from the beyond.

+++

5g

He had stayed overnight in a bland hotel in Crickhowell, where both the dinner and the wine had been tolerable, if not memorable. Having driven up from Hampshire that afternoon, he decided that it would be prudent to retire to bed early, as his ferry to Ireland left at 8am and he still had quite a few miles to drive.

Slightly to his surprise, he arrived at Fishguard with plenty of time to spare; was, in fact, second in the queue to board. He opened his window to let in some fresh sea air. The weather was calm, not too cold, and with no perceptible wind. He estimated that it should be a fairly quiet crossing to Rosslare. The water in the harbour lapped quietly at the walls. In front of him was a group of five jolly, joking Hells Angels, either sitting astride or leaning against their respective Harley-Davidson or Norton bikes. They were already clearly in holiday mode; their long, silvering hair fluttering out behind their caps and helmets, rather like the pennants on the backs of their bikes. Skull-and-crossbones motifs adorned their leather or denim jackets, while their trousers looked rather greasy.

A few more minutes to boarding, so he decided to get some air and stretch his legs. He rang Sean, as he had promised he would, just prior to getting on the ferry. They agreed to meet at 5pm in a pub in Lahinch, overlooking the beautiful Liscannor Bay in County Clare.

He was on his way back to his car when a confident, authoritarian voice hailed him from over his shoulder. 'Mr McFlynn? Ian Michael McFlynn?'

'Yes. Why?'

'We need to speak to you with regard to certain recent events in Hampshire. We have a warrant for your arrest.'

'But I need to take this ferry!'

'At the moment, sir, you are going nowhere. Furthermore, you need to accompany us to the police station in Fishguard. Now then, we can either do this the quiet and unobtrusive way, or the hard way. Which is it to be?' The arresting officer looked McFlynn beadily and meaningfully in the eye.

McFlynn sighed deeply, listened to the detective constable's brisk and by-rote recitation of his rights, and was then handcuffed and lowered into the back seat of the police car, which drove off at high speed, contravening (he noted smugly) the thirty-mile-per-hour speed limit.

+++

6a

Fingerpints were taken, forms signed, and the services of a duty solicitor offered, which McFlynn declined. A vending-machine coffee in a scalding white plastic beaker was given to him and his recorded interview commenced. He avoided the interviewing officers' steady gazes, preferring to let his eyes wander evasively around the walls and ceiling, while giving non-committal answers to their questions. After two hours of being grilled and repeated statements of 'No comment', he was placed in a cell and left to ruminate until the following morning.

A week later, DNA from the three victims was inextricably linked to samples on clothing worn by McFlynn. The police also located the murder weapon at the back of his garage: a bloodstained wooden mallet, which he had attempted to clean, but in vain. He was rearrested and placed in custody.

+++

6b

'So then,' said the detective inspector, settling into his chair, 'let's recap what we've got so far. Three young women, all in their mid-twenties, all struck fatally from behind, whose bodies were left, but not buried, in the same vicinity. The exception being the last victim, whose right eye was gouged out – hopefully, for her sake, after she was dead.'

His colleague, a detective sergeant, grimaced.

'Not nice, I agree,' said the inspector. 'However, we seem to lack a clear motive. We do know that all three victims went to the same optician's practice, though. Moreover, they were all seen by McFlynn. So there is a tentative, if loose, connection, but it still doesn't give us a reason for *why*, does it?'

They remained silent for some moments. Then the phone rang and the inspector gestured to his sergeant to leave.

Three days later, a psychological profile had been created, suggesting that the murders might well have been committed in revenge for another death, accidental or otherwise.

Ian McFlynn was interviewed again and, after much muttering and long, pregnant silences, falteringly admitted that he had taken the lives of the three young women in retribution for the death of his daughter Susan in the Boxing Day tsunami. He added that the removal of the right eye of his third victim had been as much symbolic of his profession as anything else. He also referred to the Jungian belief in balance: that the good he did as an optician needed to be balanced with opposing deeds, and that in any individual there was only a limited quantity of goodness that, after a time, would run out. He felt that this had been the case within himself, he added, after a long lacuna.

+++

6c

The court rose to its feet as the judge re-entered and the foreman of the jury stood.

'Have you reached a unanimous verdict?' asked the judge, addressing the foreman over the top of his spectacles.

'Yes, we have, Your Honour.'

'On the first count of murder, how do you find the accused?'

'Guilty.'

'On the second count of murder, how do you find the accused?'

'Guilty.'

'And finally, on the third count of murder, how do you find the accused?'

'Guilty, Your Honour.'

The judge addressed the prisoner in the dock. 'Mr McFlynn, do you have anything to say at this point?'

McFlynn, now very pale, merely shook his head.

The judge shuffled his papers together and cleared his throat loudly prior to delivering his sentence. 'Members of the jury, ladies and gentlemen. Due to the grievous and heinous nature of these crimes, I have no alternative but to convict the prisoner before me to a minimum sentence of twenty-five years. In this instance, that is all that can be said. Take him down.'

June's eyes widened and welled up. As McFlynn was led down, he glanced up at her.

The court rose and was dismissed. Reporters from local and national newspapers as well as television thronged around the court's main entrance. Amid a plethora of outstretched microphones and shouted, colliding questions, June was ushered hastily into a waiting car. Her own trial would begin shortly, as a result of which she would receive a custodial sentence of five years for perjury and contempt of court. She pleaded innocent to the charges of aiding and abetting the three murders; a plea which (to her slight surprise) was accepted by the judge and jury.

+++

6d

For the duration of his incarceration, McFlynn was a model prisoner. Every morning he worked as a librarian; a role in which he was dutiful, efficient and helpful. Over the months and years, he became slightly more sociable and – surprisingly to those who had thought they knew him – offered solace to the new and more vulnerable prisoners.

Once a month, two or three of the old faithfuls from St Boniface would visit punctiliously, and, having overcome his initial shame and embarrassment, McFlynn looked forward to their visits. These visitors did not, however, include the vicar who had prayed with McFlynn on that far-off night at the altar rail, intoning the words of '*Te Lucis Ante Terminum*'.

Each night, unbeknown to (and unheard by) the other inmates, McFlynn made afresh his confession to God in urgent whispers; sometimes accompanied by tears, sometimes not. He remembered that Latin hymn and could recite it from memory, if only to himself. It wouldn't do, particularly in that environment, to be caught praying out loud and appearing to be some kind of nutter.

In late October 2009, as the nights were drawing in and becoming darker, overnight he became blind in his right eye. No one knew how or why. A stroke was suspected, but never confirmed.

'How ironic, but deserved', was the reaction and opinion when the news seeped out.

+++

Return to **6c**.

7a

He was drifting in and out of consciousness and beginning to feel cold and clammy to the touch. It was heart failure, and one by one his organs and internal support systems were starting to switch off; his body slowing and powering down, sinking, preparing to pass on and out of this life, hopefully to something better. A cataract of thickening, cloudy film obscured his left eye.

A few hours later, the prison chaplain was summoned and arrived at McFlynn's bed within minutes, where he held his hand and quietly intoned words of comfort in a cut-glass accent, although Communion was not administered on this occasion.

McFlynn's face was drawn, hollowed and sallow; his pallor changing from greyish white to a dull, bronzy yellow; his breathing increasingly thin and laboured. The diminuendo was not to be hurried. Fifty-five minutes later, it was all over.

'Let Thy servant depart in peace, according to Your word. Amen.' The chaplain made the sign of the cross over McFlynn's forehead, bowed, and walked away to whisper some words to the ward sister.

Within minutes, the washing of the body and the completion of the paperwork would commence; then the phoning of the relatives to inform them of the time of death of their loved one – or, in this instance, their not-so-loved, barely tolerated one.

+++

7b

McFlynn, Ian Michael
2/2/1949–10/5/2010
A loved brother, always in our thoughts.
Maggie & Liam
Service at Frenswell Crematorium, Hampshire, 26th May, 11.30am.
Family flowers only, please.

+++

8a

From her home in Glasgow, Maggie spoke to the lady at the funeral parlour in McFlynn's home town.

'What would your brother have wanted?'

'No flowers. Most definitely no flowers.'

'What about music and hymns?'

Maggie, never having discussed such things with Ian, was none too sure about this. She thought that he liked Beethoven, but couldn't be entirely certain.

'Perhaps not the opening of the Fifth Symphony, then?' joked the lady, trying to lighten the tone.

'Perhaps not,' echoed Maggie through gritted teeth, thinking that this attempt at humour was inappropriate.

More questions. 'Have you thought about the type of coffin?' the woman continued.

Maggie hadn't, and said so.

'In that case, I can send you a brochure, if that's agreeable?'

It wasn't in any way agreeable, of course (how could it ever be so?), but Maggie acquiesced and then brought the conversation to a swift close. 'Well, thank you for your help. If I think of anything else, I'll ring you. Goodbye.'

She replaced the receiver without waiting for a reply, sat down and put her head in her hands. 11.30am, two weeks from tomorrow, in the crematorium five miles down the road from where her brother lived – *had* lived, she corrected herself. She walked into her kitchen and circled the date on the wall calendar.

Her husband Ronald looked up from his newspaper and sharply informed her that he had no intention whatsoever of accompanying her down south to pay his respects to 'that wee devil', as he put it. 'Pay my *respects*, hen? I had *nae* respect for the man, even if he was your brother. Not so much a brother, either – more of a burden, if you ask me.'

Which she had not, of course. But Ronald's opinion was always heard, asked for or not. Maggie shook her head, not deigning to reply, and prepared soup for their lunch. At this precise moment, she could have willingly poured a whole, steaming bowlful over his head. Instead, she made do with thumping a cupboard and uttering a couple of expletives. Even though Ronald was partially deaf and wouldn't hear it, it gave her great satisfaction to swear; yet something else of which he disapproved. She sliced some wholemeal bread and, clatteringly, fetched down a couple of side plates and bowls with as much infernal din as she could muster.

+++

Return to **3j** or **3g**.

8b

The funeral was the usual twenty-five-minute slot at the local crematorium with an officiating priest who knew nothing whatsoever of the deceased. He did manage to inject a morsel, a shred of dignity and respect into his words, although Maggie was not a believer in God, let alone any concept of an afterlife. The priest emphasised McFlynn's record as a long-serving and respected ophthalmologist, while tactfully referring to his later crimes as having been committed by an erring and weak soul who had fallen from grace following the tragic circumstances of his daughter's sudden death.

To Maggie's ears, brought up in the Kirk, it all sounded very Catholic and popish. She looked, without pleasure, around the comfortless, bland and high-windowed chapel, and at the dark wine-red velvet curtains which any moment now would be drawn shut by a mechanism activated by a switch on the priest's lectern. For some unfathomable reason, she imagined Eric Morecambe popping his head around the curtain, raising his glasses and wrinkling up his nose, before making a crack about Ernie Wise's short, hairy legs or doing that trick with the brown paper bag. She bit her lower lip and tried not to smile. Smiling at funerals tended to unsettle people; was not really wanted. After all, as the whole world already knew (thanks to the great and glorious media machine), her brother had done nothing to smile about. The exact opposite, in fact.

Cremation – another word for processing as many bodies as they could decently (indecently) dispose of each day. A sausage-factory-style process, basically. Maggie thought of how Ian had liked his sausages – if not exactly cremated and blackened, then at least very well done. The staff, creeping around in their black suits, feigning sympathy and respect, and talking in lowered voices, while sending out the grossly inflated bill. How dare they? All Masons to a man, thought Maggie bitterly, loathing the artificiality and connivance of the entire death industry. However much the whole thing was softened or the infernal pill sugared, death was a business; nothing more and nothing less. Bloody hypocrites.

Including Maggie herself, and June (handcuffed to two female prison guards), there were only five mourners, or three if you discounted the guards, who were obliged to be present – not wishing to be there, of course, but doing their job, their so-called duty. As if she's going to attempt to make a run for it at her lover's funeral, thought Maggie, sighing at the ludicrousness of the situation and shaking her head in disbelief. Her other brother Liam had opted not to attend. The one remaining person was unknown to Maggie: a younger man who, despite the priest's invitation to come forward, shook his head and insisted on remaining a few pews back from the two female mourners. Maggie had to restrain herself from perpetually glancing over her shoulder at him or glaring sideways at June. The man's face was totally unfamiliar. Who was he?

There were no flowers on the coffin. McFlynn had always loathed flowers; thought them useless in comparison to growing useful vegetables in his small garden. Everything was austere and unadorned. It was only afterwards that Maggie realised how appropriate this was to her brother's life and character. Photos from their childhood kept flashing into her mind: beach holidays in North Wales; a lanky and unsmiling Ian with his hands behind his back, not quite looking at the camera. Formal and remote, even back then.

It had always been hard, if not well-nigh impossible, to know what he was thinking. Yes, a hidden personality, definitely. But, come to think of it, not a great deal of personality, truth be told. And the truth *should* be told at a time like this, she reflected. And not just what the tabloids had printed, either.

A bare twenty-three minutes later they filed out of the chapel to the usual cloying piped music and departed without speaking; Maggie being ushered into the back seat of the undertaker's black limousine by a slightly unctuous, bowing funeral director. She had noticed the bored-looking superintendent of the crematorium glancing surreptitiously (but not surreptitiously enough) at his watch; the unfeeling, officious grey-haired bastard. Meanwhile, the unfamiliar young man had vanished, seemingly into thin air; as if he had never been there; as if he had been a feathery spectre at the non-feast.

There was no post-funeral wake, mercifully sparing the four assembled stomachs the expected dreary cold collation of sausage rolls, ham sandwiches, and something faintly spicy, plus the obligatory cherry tomatoes, limp sticks of celery, and other apologies for buffet food, all served in an inadequately heated back room of a pub with a dismal (already funereal) atmosphere. With so few mourners and June having to be escorted immediately back to prison, there had seemed no point; no point at all.

+++

Return to **6c**.

8c

So that was it, then. Done and dusted. Earth to earth, dust to dust, ashes to ashes. Something like that. At any rate, Ian Michael McFlynn was no more, and if he was meeting his Maker face to face he was, presumably, squirming in his chair as his long list of offences against humanity was read out, in a stentorian voice, by some higher authority such as an archangel. Or perhaps he was being made to stand throughout this ordeal which droned on, hour after interminable hour, day after insufferable day.

Perhaps, though, there were neither chairs nor clock time in heaven; just eternity? Given that the physical body had gone, given up the ghost and been burned beyond recognition, legs wouldn't now, presumably, be needed by McFlynn, wherever he was currently residing. A suitably humbling and humiliating punishment for his earthly misdemeanours, no doubt. If there was a God, He would be sorting Ian out, Maggie felt certain. That much she believed, at least. An eye for an eye and all that. Yes, how ironic was that? Very, given his profession. Very biblical too, aye. She thought of the old Irish tune 'Avenging and Bright'. Her brother had done more than his fair share of avenging in the past year or so, that was for sure. But now he, in his turn, had been mightily (Almightily) avenged.

Maggie nodded involuntarily at the thought.

+++

8d

And I saw a new heaven and a new earth: for the first heaven and the first earth were passed away; and there was no more sea…

And God shall wipe away all tears from their eyes; and there shall be no more death, neither sorrow, nor crying, neither shall there be any more pain: for the former things are passed away.

(Revelation 21, vv. 1 and 4)

No more sea, no more tears. Beautiful, but surely not true? No, not true at all, she pondered. How could it be so, in our fragile and fractious lifetime on earth? Time and life. Time as a prison with no life whatsoever. Time dragging, therefore life dragging, too.

In her cell, June carefully laid down her inscribed copy of the New Testament and Psalms (presented on the final day of her final summer term in junior school) and began to write her diary entry for the day.

…neither sorrow, nor crying…

Come on, girl. No more tears now, she thought sternly, reaching for a tissue. Tomorrow morning was visiting time and her lad was coming to see her. She picked up her biro and wrote hurriedly in a neat and tiny script, not stopping until she reached the bottom of the page, as thoughts raced and tumbled out of her aching brain.

+++

Return to **4b**, *then* **6c**.

8e

When the rebuilding programme started and life gradually began to return to what it had been before the tsunami, Bethari and Raharjo resumed their schooling, albeit in different classes. In another few years, they would both study at the senior school.

In the November of their final year, it was announced during the school assembly that the much-loved and wise Father Egan O'Flaherty had died. The cause was not given, though the adults present suspected that it was most probably alcohol-related. He had been admitted to the hospital some weeks earlier. Virtually the entire population of the island turned out to celebrate his life and work, both at the funeral and afterwards at the wake, where copious amounts of alcohol were consumed. The old boy would have wanted it no other way; was probably looking down and nodding in approval. Those who remembered his short lesson on the special word now hoped that he had indeed achieved the state of *iklas*.

Bethari and Raharjo remained inseparable and, in due time, became lovers.

After completing their respective university courses in Australia, they married and returned to the island as teachers, eventually funding the building of their own school in memory of their parents and the others who had died. The school bore their surname, as, did their two children: a boy and, two years later, a girl.

There would, naturally, be other tsunamis and disasters around the neighbouring islands, but their new school stood firm, constructed as it was in the shelter of inland hills and on firm ground. Their family also remained firm and grounded, and their children were much treasured.

+++

Return to **4e**, *then* **3k**.

9a

Five days after the funeral, McFlynn's sister Maggie was going through his things, putting his clothes and other (now unwanted) items into black plastic bags for the local charity shops. She calculated that the whole unpleasant business would not take too long (maybe a couple of days), as he had not been overly keen on possessions, had been tidy in his habits, and, mercifully, had not been a hoarder. Her husband, Ronald, had not accompanied her on this trip; indeed, had not wanted to know about it at all. She felt annoyed at this but, in all honesty, had not expected anything else.

At the back of the right-hand side of the high shelf in the wardrobe, she found a bundle of letters held together by elastic bands. She removed the bands and glanced at the top letter, which was dated from many years ago. Written in ink in a small, neat hand, the writing had faded but was still legible. The letters were from Ian's first wife. Beneath them was a small, quite heavy medal with a navy-blue striped ribbon. Maggie put on her glasses and read the inscription. It had been awarded to Ian during his ophthalmic studies for being the most brilliant and gifted student in his year. Around the rim of the medal, the words (they were hard to make out) said something about it being awarded by the Royal Society or some such august institution. At any rate, he had never, ever mentioned it; had probably forgotten all about it himself. She held it in her hand a moment and then placed it gently at the bottom of her handbag. The charity shops were not having this item.

That was enough; all she could cope with for today. She quietly closed the bedroom door, tiptoed down the stairs as if she were an intruder in her brother's house, and let herself out, remembering to lock the front door behind her. She would have to steel herself to come back tomorrow and then face the long drive back up the motorways to Glasgow, with all those black bags in the boot and on the back seats of her car. It might be better, she pondered, to dispose of them locally.

Once in the car she sat for a few minutes to compose herself, then took a deep breath, looked briefly in the rear-view mirror, released the handbrake and drove off back to the hotel.

+++

9b

As Maggie drove, the unsmiling face of the young man from the crematorium floated back into her mind and swam around in there for a wee while. Unfamiliar, and yet…

+++

9c

She tried to imagine the moonlight on the beach in Bali; its brilliant whiteness.

Also the velvety, moonless dark of the Hampshire churchyard; its patches of thick, cushiony moss and the dank smell of sodden earth.

+++

9d

The next day, her task was done. Maggie dropped off the bags at three charity shops in Hampshire, returned the rear seats of her car to their upright positions, and set off on the long haul north to Glasgow.

The clouds were gradually dispersing and a pallid sun was attempting, feebly, to shine through the dissipating rain. In a field on her left side, half a rainbow arced steeply from the dewy grass and then disappeared abruptly into dark grey cloud. Moments later, a thinner echo of the first (main) rainbow appeared alongside it, following the trajectory of the first. A double rainbow! Heavens, she hadn't witnessed one of those in years; possibly decades!

Suddenly, that array of chromatic colours felt like a positive sign; a strengthening; a good, hopeful omen; and almost involuntarily she began to accelerate towards home. She glanced in the rear-view mirror and, to her surprise (and after everything that had happened), she was smiling. Even the thought of Glasgow and returning to curmudgeonly Ronald felt almost bearable. More than anything else now, she wanted to be at home. She put her foot down confidently on the accelerator as she joined the motorway from the descending slip road.

+++

9e

The clouds had now dispersed and there was a feeling of brightness in the air. Despite the buffeting wind, Maggie was sure that she heard the song of a blackbird. To her ears it sounded like a kind of praise or rejoicing; as if a heavy weight had been irrevocably (and unexpectedly) lifted from her. An intolerable burden raised from her shoulders; expelled from her mind and from all of her body.

In those moments, Maggie felt helped; by whom, she could not be sure, but she was hugely and mightily grateful. A return, yes; yet a new beginning, too. An elliptical journey.

The traffic was flowing steadily and she was nearly over the border now. A few miles to the north, a strong sun lit up the dark hills of her childhood, as if in welcome and greeting; as if acknowledging her return.

+++

9f

Maggie unlocked the front door. She had barely stepped into the hallway before Ronald was there, proffering a small glass of whisky in one hand and a small bunch of red roses in the other.

'Och, I've missed you so much, hen,' he said, embracing her with the strength of an old, slightly battered, yet still-proud lion. The beginnings of a tear formed in his right eye. 'Aye. Welcome home. Come and have some lunch.'

Then he led her into the kitchen, where he ladled out two generous bowls of steaming Scotch broth. Thickly buttered oatcakes were already on the side plates. They raised their soup spoons to their lips, almost in a simultaneous toast.

'It's good to be home,' said Maggie, nodding and smiling.

Ronald smiled back with relief. 'Well, it wasn't the same without you. How could it ever be?' he said gently, reaching across and laying his gnarled, age-spotted hand over hers.

They held the moment, as steam rose from their bowls of broth, seemingly in unison. It was an unlooked-for and unexpected, yet gratefully received, epiphany.

+++

9g

Once again the young man's face floated weightlessly in Maggie's line of vision and lingered for a moment. This time he was smiling.

+++

9h

Bethari gave birth, safely and successfully, to her third child, a boy, whom in a day or so she and Raharjo would name Iklas Egan, in honour and remembrance of the widely loved Father O'Flaherty and that lesson, learned so long ago, that haunted them still.

+++

Return to **4j**, *then* **3o**.

9i

But that isn't, necessarily, the end of the story.

For there will always remain ghosts and those numerous echoes that cannot, should not and will not be forgotten by the living; the ones who are left and who have to live, no matter what, suffering and bearing the brunt, the stains, the strains and the multitudinous consequences of death. Those clamouring, hammering memories that outlive and outstay the flesh; even the bones.

+++

9j

'People are apt to say that life is too short,' wrote June in her diary after dinner one evening, when the rain was lashing vehemently against the small, high, dirty window of her cell. 'No, it's not. It's not too bloody short at all. That is sentimental nonsense. Life is not short enough and often feels far too intolerably bloody long, believe me. But only if you want to believe me, of course, and, in a certain sense, after all that has happened, why should you? Indeed, if anyone ever gets to read this.'

She raised her eyebrows and pursed her lips at the irony of that penultimate sentence. With good behaviour, she might be out in a year or two, or so she reckoned.

The grille in the door of her cell shot up with a ricocheting, metallic bang, and made June jump, as it always did. An unsmiling, hard-etched female face with too much black mascara and chalky face powder stared in at her, before slamming the grille back down almost petulantly, as if in a bad temper. A bad-tempered panda and an echoing miniature guillotine.

'Fucking cow,' muttered June under her breath, as she continued to scribble fast.

Nine months later, almost to the day, June was found hanged in her cell. After Ian's death, there had been nothing left to live for, even her son, and she simply hadn't seen the point of it; the point of any of it whatsoever.

+++

Finish here, or return to **1b** *and then* **9f**.

Acknowledgements

Colin McPhee's *A House in Bali* (OUP, 1986);
Gavin Francis's *Adventures in Human Being* (Profile Books, Wellcome Collection, 2016);
Jennifer Lindsay's *Javanese Gamelan* (OUP, 1979).

Ellipsis

Do not because this day I have grown saturnine
Imagine that lost love, inseparable from my thought
Because I have no other youth, can make me pine;
For how should I forget the wisdom that you brought,
The comfort that you made?
(From 'Under Saturn' by W. B. Yeats)

1

Ellipsis...ellipses...connotations and variations of absence, cavity (dentists drilling teeth; discomfort and pain), discontinuity (of space-time; warps), gap, hole (sinkholes suddenly opening up; houses disappearing into the earth), lacuna, opening, void (endless as in outer space; or null and...).

What's this book about, you may be asking?

Reflections, really. Small reflections, ponderings, soliloquies: on absences, both small and large; momentary snapshots caught and suspended in mid-air. That is what this book is about (or attempts to be about), yes.

2

'Joe! *Joe?!*'

'I'm over here. Who's that?'

'Uncle Jack. Where are you? I can barely see the hands in front of my face...'

'Over here.'

'Damn this fog...'

'Over here, Jack...'

'Joe?'

'Jack?'

...

3

Northern France, First World War

Thousands of their mates and comrades, shot by snipers through gaps in sandbags, or blown sky-high into pieces…mines in no man's land…limbs and other mutilated bits of bodies rained down, resembling an anarchic butcher's shop…

The crucifying barbed wire (crown of thorns), and always the mud, the insufferable mud…

…

The stench of faeces and urine, decaying bodies…

Ankle-deep, boot-deep in piss, shit and putrefaction…worse than any zoo or abattoir…

Narrow trenches; mere deep-sided gullies, really. Barely room to pass two abreast…

Latrine; interesting word – sounds French, if not quite exotic. *La Trine* – definitely not a harpsichord piece by one of the Couperin dynasty or Rameau. Although it sounds as if it should be or could be.

But I shouldn't jest; not in the same (dying) breath as those soldiers in their filthy uniforms and conditions, poor sods…

Clods of earth, sods of the earth…terra firma, their final resting place…

The incessant rain practically drowned them, turned their trenches into moats, but without the castles…peace, like some forlorn hope out of reach; the unreal dream. Castles in the air…

They have all vanished or will disappear, bent and hunched, those khaki ghosts in the cold morning mists…

Tin hats riddled with holes; drying streams of blood…

Gloves through which poke the remnants of hands which once belonged to a beating heart; a caressing father, son, lover…yes, caress and sing…

Mustard gas, choke-retch, burned eyes…empty eye sockets…

The whooshing of shells…the infernal racket of all of this…

Mental/physical trauma; nightmares for the rest of their lives…

Oh, oh, oh dear…odious…our odour us…

Sometimes, if the wind was blowing in the right direction, you could smell their pipe smoke wafting over no man's land…

Send reinforcements, we're going to advance.
Send three-and-fourpence, we're going to a dance.

HAIG

Horrendous!	**A**gonising!	**I**'m	**G**uilty!
Horrible!	**A**dmonish!		**G**ruesome!
Humiliating!	**A**bhorrent!		**G**reedy
Hypercritical!	**A**bet	**I**mperialism!	**G**as gangrene
Hatred!	**A**bandoned	**I**gnoble	**G**odforsaken
Haemorrhage	**A**bdicate	**I**gnorant	**G**roan
Hernia	**A**bominable!		
Havoc	**A**bnegate	**I**mmovable	
Hoar frost	**A**cquiesce	**I**nfernal	

Hogwash	**A**damant	**I**ntercept
	Agitation	**I**ntransigent
	Ambush	
	Amputation	
	Atonement	

Such an awful catalogue, that outpouring of negatives…

Think long and hard enough about this and you will need a dram of whisky; possibly one with the same damned name. But I very much doubt that the whisky (any whisky) ever maimed and slaughtered the equivalent number of soldiers (lest we forget: human beings, not guinea pigs) as did that supreme bastard of a general…

Lest we forget…but we do: we *do* forget; we always *bloody* well *do* forget. Don't we?

4

'I've got to go now,' he said, pulling on his trousers and zipping himself up. He combed his hair perfunctorily.

'Yes, that's right, you go,' she said, sounding resentful. He'd had his way with her and now he couldn't wait to get off. Get off back to his other life, meaning his wife; the part that she couldn't know or be part of. That seventy-five, eighty per cent that was fully lived, yet hidden from her.

She pulled up her black tights slowly, carefully. She had probed him a little about his wife, but he had refused to be drawn, except for a few non-committal mumblings along the lines of 'You wouldn't understand.'

'Try me,' she had said, just that once, several months ago near the start of it all, stubbing out her cigarette in the ashtray. But he'd merely gestured lamely, with a barely perceptible raising of his shoulders; or looked away and changed the subject.

A look of stalemate passed between them now, and he looked out of the window, avoiding her face. Then, as if to make amends, and sensing that, in some unintended way, he had hurt her, he quickly lit another cigarette and passed it to her. They stared at the once-white, now beige-yellow Artex ceiling stained with nicotine. Smoke drifted, coiled up lazily...hanging, suspended heavily, in the extended silence that lay between them...

...

5

On 22 January 1901, Queen Victoria died. She had been a widow for some forty years (like Clara Schumann), and seemingly never stopped grieving for her late husband Albert. An epic absence.

This absence, this loneliness as large as a planet, dominated her wherever she went, dragging in her wake like a heavy black train on an otherwise white wedding dress. The black and the white together created a deep and sombre shade of dark grey.

This planet slowly, laboriously orbited in great darkness; took many years to complete one cycle. The darkness seemed to permeate and suffuse her homes, such as her beloved Osborne House on the then-fashionable Isle of Wight. Definitely an austere abode, as I remember when I visited it on holiday when I was eighteen. A deep gloom was the abiding impression.

Abide with me; fast falls the eventide;
The darkness deepens; Lord, with me abide…[3]

Those last forty years without him must have seemed an eternal evening to her. No wonder that she looked so glum and sour:

---

3 The composer of that hymn-tune was W. H. Monk (1823–89), one of the finest hymn writers of his age. The words are by H. F. Lyte (1793–1847).

her head hung low; those rather bulbous, vacant eyes…a mixture of grief and thyroid trouble?

She was born on 24 May 1819 and reigned for sixty-three years, seven months and two days. She married Albert on 10 February 1840 in the Chapel Royal of St James's Palace and bore her husband nine children. Ten Prime Ministers served under her, some of whom served two or more (non-consecutive) terms in office.

In March 1861, Victoria's mother died and there was intense grief and, doubtless, a sense of guilt on Victoria's part, as for many years she had been convinced that her mother had never loved her. At the beginning of December of that year, Albert was very unwell and was diagnosed as having typhoid fever, by no less a person than the esteemed scientist William Jenner. Albert's health worsened and he died on 14 December.

An inconsolable Victoria now entered a prolonged state of mourning, and for the remainder of her life wore nothing but black. A black widow – but did she weave webs of intrigue?

On 30 July 1900, her second son Alfred died. She wrote in her diary, it was 'a horrible year, nothing but sadness and horrors of one kind and another.' She would have just under six months left to live.

6

The Blitz, East End of London, 1940

Craters, debris, dust and smoke everywhere you looked. Dust in your eyes, mouth and nostrils, too. Gaps where houses had once stood – like teeth knocked out by a boxer. A heavyweight, remorseless aerial boxer called the Luftwaffe.

'Can't go any further, I'm afraid, love. Too dangerous after last night.' An ARP warden, tin hat tilted back on his head, face streaked with grime, stood resolute, his right hand held up like a policeman's.

'Is number 19 all right? Could you check?' She thought that she already knew the answer.

'Will do, but you must stay here. It's not safe.' He walked away, lethargic and languorous. He had probably been up most of the night. After what seemed an eternity, he came back a few minutes later. 'Not good news, love. The house is down,' he said apologetically, raising his eyebrows in a gesture of sympathy.

'Are Alf and Doris all right?'

'What's their surname?'

'Winters.'

He consulted a list, flicking over a couple of pages. 'Wadham… Walsh… West… Here we are – Winters.'

A momentary silence, which to her seemed very prolonged.

'Yes, they caught the blast a bit, but have been taken to the local hospital. They were able to walk to the ambulance, but I don't know anything more. Hopefully, nothing too serious.'

'Oh God. Thank you so much. That's a great relief.' She shook her head, as if shaking away an apparition.

'Relations?'

'Yes, my parents.'

'Well, good luck, love.' He saluted her and smiled.

The early morning mist was beginning to lift and she was going to go to the hospital now, right away, before the commencement of her busy day...

7

One morning he woke up, not knowing where he was. He had dreamed, yet again, of being shot in the back; the bullet roaring through and searing out the front of his stomach. He felt sudden pain and stickiness. He glanced down and saw that there was a small, yet very bloody hole where the bullet had escaped.

He tried hard to open his eyes. He was lying on his right side. Gingerly, through semi-open eyes, he looked around him. All was quiet; no guns going off. He was in bed, not on the battlefield. There was no blood, thank God – Eileen wouldn't have been too pleased about that. The sweats were bad enough. Sometimes the sheets needed to be washed daily, and he felt bad about that: more work for his lass, his devoted wife. The dream was always the same: incessant, over and over, even though this was 1925.

His head had been resting on his right arm, which was now quite stiff. He raised the arm, flexing it slightly, then lowered it in front of his face. He could hear his wife moving around downstairs. Monday morning. She would be in her pinny, doing the washing. Quite fetching, actually. He eyed the sandy hairs on his forearm. Up close, they resembled tanned or rusting barbed wire.

In a mere moment, he was back there. Barbed wire and too many mines. He tried to block out the thoughts of Bill, who, only a few minutes before, had been lighting a cigarette a few feet away from him in the trench. Bill, who had stepped on a mine and been, literally, blown almost sky-high. It could have been him, or any one of them, come to that. That was the part that hurt; that nagged at him and eroded any peace. The ensuing seconds had taken an age, had been prolonged, and had seemed to occur out of time, as the men looked away, but imagined Bill's body parts landing, scattered, over a wide area. Stumps of limbs lay around; fractured, smeared faces, like something out of a hellish Bosch painting, but with the various stenches as a hideous bonus – if, that is, that could be called a bonus. He and Bill had been close; had grown up in the same part of the Yorkshire Dales; had known the same people, eaten the same food and drunk the same ale. Such seemingly simple things bonded men together. Now, there was just this huge gap; a prolonged hollow in the pit of his stomach. Just this…justice? How could anyone in their right mind call this justice?

As always, he felt exhausted, but slowly swung his feet out of bed, just sitting on the edge in his faded striped pyjamas. Both the jacket and the trousers were covered in sweat. He fervently wished that his memories would fade. Without moving, he stared blankly at the wall, trying to empty his mind. He wiped away tears with the backs of both hands. His wife called up to see if he was all right and wanted some breakfast. Yes, thanks, he was and he did, but time for a wash and a shave first. He hated the idea of breakfasting while unshaven. He felt a little light-headed, so steadied himself as he made his way to the bathroom. He found it difficult to look in the mirror; to see the gaunt reflection of a man who had been irrevocably changed, as had all of his generation. To see a shadow of the man who had married his sweetheart, back in the early summer of 1914.

A few minutes later, freshly washed, shaven, and with hair combed and brilliantined, he came downstairs in open-necked shirt and braces to the smell of bacon and the sound of frying eggs spitting and spluttering in the large pan on the stove. There was a fresh, steaming brown pot of tea placed in front of where he sat. He kissed his wife and sat down. Over the hills, seen from the kitchen window of their cottage, clouds were scudding hither and thither, while the sun was strengthening in its power.

It could almost be a normal world, he thought, gently replacing his cup in its saucer. But he knew that it wasn't; that it was purely an illusion, a mirage of the mind. He watched the smoke drift up lazily, away from the chimney of the cottage just below their field. At least that was real. He laid his knife and fork down neatly together in the middle of the plate, stepped outside and lit a cigarette, standing on the back doorstep.

8

'Jack?!'

Silence.

'Jack!'

Slight pause. 'Who's that?'

'Joe. It's Joe, your nephew. You know – me, Joe. Speak to me, Uncle Jack!'

Then Jack's voice, flat and blanketed, as if it were coming from a tremendous distance: 'Go away, Joe. I'm not ready for you. It's not your time. Go back! Now!'

His voice felt nearer now, almost booming and resonating through the fog which was beginning to thin out into curling clouds of mist. There was absolutely no doubting his message; that commanding voice…

9

Yes, it's something I have never forgotten and would never wish to forget.

I was having a particularly severe asthma attack. I was lying on the bed and things started to fade; to go blank. Uh-oh, I thought, this isn't looking good. Actually, old son, this could be curtains for you. I definitely remember thinking that, you know: that this could be it and my time was up.

The next thing I knew, I was hovering, suspended in mid-air, looking down at my own struggling body. At that moment my secondary body – the one that had lifted up to the ceiling – felt incredibly light, as if it weighed practically nothing at all. Oddly enough, I wasn't worried. And time seemed to have stopped; to be, like my body, in a state of suspension. Directly ahead, as well as above and all around me, was a blinding white, rotating light which was pulsing very strongly. It was hypnotic, and I had to resist the powerful temptation to submit to it and be drawn in. It also appeared to contain all the colours of the rainbow, yet its radiance seemed to be this extraordinarily intense and pure whiteness. I remember thinking, Unfold my wings, so that I might fly away from all this, all this pain. For a few moments, or maybe just the one prolonged moment, I think that I actually did just that.

Then I felt a jolt and realised that I had re-entered my body. Cautiously, I opened my eyes. I was lying on top of the bed and my asthma attack was virtually gone. Sunlight streamed in through the open window. There was a slight breeze wafting in, and it was only then that I realised that I was alive, but had very nearly been drawn through and beyond the gates of death. It was a thoroughly chilling realisation, but I felt gratitude for having survived it.

I shivered, put on my dressing gown, and gingerly stepped over to close the window.

10

VE Day, May 1945

She was dancing gaily in a long line, snaking in and out, shaking it all around and about Trafalgar Square. Total strangers shook hands and hugged one another. Piped music, balloons, streamers, many kisses and much laughter. For the first time in six years, church bells rang freely and in celebration, rather than as a warning of imminent invasion.

There was still rubble and flattened buildings everywhere, but the mood was one of glorious victory. Beforehand, in her office, one of her colleagues had been glum, but trying against the odds to put a brave face on things. For her, this felt like a rather false celebration, as her fiancé was still abroad fighting the Japanese, but inwardly she was happy for her friends, although she found it hard to smile, laugh, or show any emotion at all.

The snaking line grew ever longer, comprising civilians and soldiers and sailors. People wore party hats, blew toy trumpets, waved and danced in a seemingly endless sea of smiles. Windows on the top decks of buses were thrown open and passengers shouted out to all and sundry in a carillon of joy. The four lions were covered with people waving flags and singing boisterously. Most people were caught up in the rejoicing and wished that this could continue for ever and a day. Not even the gayest party had ever been a match for this.

She bumped into a man, who smiled broadly back at her and held her gaze for a moment. His face was familiar. Without his tin hat, it took her a moment to recognise him. Of course! The thoughtful ARP warden from five years earlier, who had checked that her parents were still alive. What was the likelihood of this? After a few words, they embraced. Yes, they were both still single. Would she like to go for a drink with him sometime? You know, given the prevailing mood up West and all that. They exchanged names and addresses on the backs of old Tube tickets (luckily, he had a stub of pencil in his pocket) and agreed to meet the next day.

They walked out, became engaged, and two years later they married and she moved into his house, bearing him their first child, a sturdy boy with large blue eyes (just like his father) and curly blond hair (like her), a year and a half later.

11

They had spent that Sunday afternoon at her place, drinking white wine (an apricoty Viognier), and had made love twice; the last time slower and more giving on his behalf. The first time had been a pure, urgent screw; the second was sensual, caressing, and lasted about three times as long. Then they drifted off into a light doze, their limbs entangled.

After that second time, after their light sleep, she had placed her left hand on his chin, turned it towards her face and asked him if he loved her. He frowned for a moment; looked puzzled. What did she mean? Of course he did; what a silly question. But he avoided looking her directly in the eye. But did he still adore her?

He pretended to not hear that. He sat bolt upright on the bed. 'I must go,' he said, pulling on underpants and socks.

The usual stale and predictable mantra, she thought. 'Yes, I know. Back to your little wife, your *normal* life and all that jazz.' Her voice sounded tight. She managed a sour, grimacing smile, while watching him dress, then comb his hair.

'She's not little. She's quite tall, actually.' He sounded defensive.

He bent over her, but kissed her perfunctorily on the forehead, not the mouth. She would remember this, after it had all finished between them. That non-kiss, and the vacant, elsewhere look in his eyes.

Then he was out the door and she could hear his abrupt yet light footsteps clattering on the stairs, as if he were relieved to be away and gone. Almost a kind of tap dance, but no Fred Astaire…

Gone and away…which, within only a few days, would irrevocably become 'gone away'…

12

If ours is not the reason to know why,
Then forgive us if we sob, weep or cry,
Before the light fades and we say goodbye…

13

That first time, no one, not a single person, told me what to expect.

From the consultant downwards, the staff were just coldly efficient, but unconcerned, and I was left in turmoil; in an unreachable black pit. You never, ever forget that; that and the physical coldness of the jelly being applied to your belly. A long silence, then the frown of the nurse, and then the absence, the plunging absence of a heartbeat...

It occurred almost exactly seven weeks to the day after conception, and totally without warning. There were terrible cramps which made me double up in agony, and I thought I was going to be violently sick, too. I only just got to the loo in time, for then the foetus and the other remains came out in a fast and very bloody torrent. I must have been in there for half an hour, waiting for it to stop, unable to look down into the bowl, and afraid that if I pulled up my knickers and flushed it away, it would start all over again.

I was at home, and my husband was there, but he was as terrified as I was. He made me a cup of tea, put his arms around me, gave my shoulders an affectionate squeeze, and tried to help, but... Over the next few weeks, I didn't want to talk about it and he didn't have the words, so it was a kind of stalemate, really. A complete void. I was glad to have him around, obviously, but... What words could there be, anyway? What can ever replace a lost child?

If it had been a girl, we were going to call her Serena; if a boy, then Christopher Michael.

For many weeks afterwards, everything seemed pointless and irrelevant. We groped through the days like zombies. If he/she had gone to full term, he/she would have been a late Scorpio or an early Sagittarius...

It sounds daft, but what made a huge difference were the lemon-scented roses in the garden, which I went out to sniff each morning after a tiny breakfast (I couldn't get much to stay down for a while), and listening to the penultimate track on KT Tunstall's first album *Eye to the Telescope*. It was track eleven, 'Heal Over', and I played that again and again; pretty obsessively, really. It was, in effect, the soundtrack to my life at that point, and, yes, it did begin to heal not just me, but both of us. It seemed a near-miracle at the time; a kind of blessing, as if we were being watched over and held in some kind of protective embrace.

Well, two years later we tried again, with the same awful result. Except that, this time, there was a tiny portion of the foetus left, about as big (or as small) as my thumbnail. Yes – left clinging high up, after the awful evacuation. As if it hadn't wanted to relinquish life; or, at least, the (if only temporary) possibility of life. As if to say, 'Don't forget me.' As if we ever could or would, of course...

Me...don't forget...me...

Forgive me, my unknown darling...

14

Yes, they are still there, watching over us; beyond the unseen veil, floating in their own dimension; a dimension and mode of pure spirit, as yet unknown to us, but to be revealed later and all in good time…their time, not ours…

15

With the seemingly indivisible union of sea and sky, you feel as if you are in Cornwall. Except that, as you descend the steep hill and then drive over the hump bridge into the small village of Aberdaron, you are in north-west and wholly Welsh-speaking Wales. Driving along the narrow lanes in summer with the car windows open, you smell the fragrant coconut wafting of gorse in abundance and you sense that you really are elsewhere; far out on the end of a remote and ancient land. And you would be entirely correct, for you are on the Llŷn (Lleyn) Peninsula, with its many and virtually deserted beaches, such as Porth Ceiriad, with its imposing, stratified red cliffs.

Out beyond the treacherous six-knot currents and tide races of Bardsey Sound lies the distant humpback-whale shape of Ynys Enlli, better known to English birdwatchers as Bardsey, the south-western island that is battered by the fierce Irish Sea. Here you will see and hear the raucous kittiwakes, other gulls, shearwaters, guillemots, shags and cormorants defending their patch and their nests in the crags of the cliffs.

Since medieval times, if not before, this has been a place of pilgrimage. Indeed, once upon a time, three pilgrimages to Ynys Enlli were considered to be the equivalent of one trip to Rome for those devout souls intent on masochistic hardship. The bucking, tossing boats and the seasickness might have had something to do with that reasoning. A pilgrimage is not meant to be easy, is it? The 'grim' portion of that word is, therefore, very apt.

A religious community was founded in c. 516 AD by Cadfan and, according to legend, some twenty thousand saints were buried here. That's a lot of remains (however holy) on an island that only measures a mile and a half long by a mile wide... A monastery was built in the early seventh century and gave shelter to a thousand monks.

In later centuries, Bardsey also served as a refuge for pirates, and many ships foundered on its jagged rocks, their assorted cargoes being requisitioned by the aforesaid brigands (or 'dodgy geezers' in modern parlance).

July 1984

It had been a very odd day indeed; one which the locals wouldn't forget in a hurry.

At one farm near Botwnnog, at lunchtime the farmer had been sitting on his wall talking to a neighbour, when he was pitched clean off it by the sudden, jolting movement of the earth underneath him, accompanied by a sound like thunder or a roaring and ripping. A visiting organist in Nefyn church was playing a Bach fugue, when he thought he had drawn the thirty-two-foot tuba stop by mistake, there seemed to be so much rumbling and shaking.

Then, much later that day, towards midnight, this other bizarre event occurred; witnessed by at least a dozen people from either on or near the beach at Aberdaron.

At the hotel overlooking the beach, the landlady and her husband had put the bar to bed and locked up. As she was about to draw their bedroom curtains, she glanced over to Ynys Enlli and saw what seemed to be a large white cloud ascending very slowly, directly above the island. She mentioned this to her husband, and he fetched his binoculars. They took turns to look at this mysterious phenomenon, while wondering aloud what it might be. As their eyes became accustomed to the darkness, it was clear that the cloud contained images of angels or saints. Many upturned faces, too many to number, and all with their hands raised in front of their faces in an attitude of prayer. The cloud lifted higher and higher, until it faded silently out of sight.

The next morning, he brought her a cup of tea in bed. While she was reading, he stole down to the cellar to check one or two things. He switched on the torch. Yes, it was all there. In the farthest corner, secreted behind a couple of barrels, were the timers and the explosives wrapped in old sheets. He must phone the boys tonight. All was set for Wednesday. He rubbed his hands, turned off the torch, and walked back up the stairs.

16

What you must realise is that nothing remains permanent. All things pass and are transient; even the worst woes of our fractured world…

17

She had decided, on the spur of the moment, to make them a picnic, and they would drive out to their favourite place, remote and away from the hustle and bustle of the city. Ham rolls, gherkins, hard-boiled eggs, tomatoes, apples and pears, ginger beer, a small flagon of cider (for him), and the obligatory, traditional tartan rug without which no proper picnic was complete. A lunch fit for a king and queen, eaten overlooking their private kingdom.

The hills had a panoramic 180-degree view over and into the adjacent county. Apart from a handful of sheep in the distance, no one was here. There were no clouds, either; just an unending sky of cerulean blue. Here was their land where, just for an hour or two, no one could disturb them in their intimacy.

With ill temper she gathered together the remains of the picnic, virtually threw the hamper into the boot of the car, then slammed it shut. The metallic echo resonated around the hills. She let out the clutch and roared off, neither of them speaking during the awkward journey home.

She dropped him off outside his house, revving the engine to drown out his apologies and pleas for her to come in.

'I'm going, you bastard,' was all she said, looking at him daggers, and then she drove off with squealing tyres.

An hour later, she phoned him to say that it was all over between them. He was too shocked to respond; thus only confirming and deepening her opinion of him as a cowardly shit who didn't remotely deserve her.

18

'For those first few weeks, none of us were allowed to see him. The nearest we got was peering anxiously through the window of his room, where he was being kept in isolation. We waved, but for many a long day he didn't wave back. We tried to keep strong, both for him and for ourselves, but it was a huge struggle. We often prayed, and sometimes that brought a little comfort and relief, but not all the time. There were many days when God seemed not to be listening, or was just being cussed and deliberately ignoring us. Aye, we know He's very busy, but all the same…

'Often, we felt as if we were walking around with concrete in our shoes, we felt that heavy. The tubes in him seemed legion and to be sprouting out from him everywhere. No, he didn't move at all; just lay there with his eyes closed, looking like some machine or robot. For six of those nine weeks, he was in an induced coma. The doctors and nurses were brilliant and devoted in their care, but no one could predict if he would pull through. Then, all of a sudden, he opened his eyes and seemed to turn a corner, day by slow day.

'And now, at long last, he's home, thank God. Who would have ever thought it, eh? We've been married thirty years but, I tell you, for most of those nine weeks I was convinced that I was going to be a widow. Aye, his appetite is slowly returning and he's got a bit of colour in his cheeks, bless him. Slowly but surely, eh? He's delighted to be home, aren't you, love? Come on, time for your rest and your tablets. Up you go. D' you want an arm? You can watch the snooker later. He's got that many tablets, he'll be rattling with every step soon, right enough. Won't you, sweetheart?'

She leaned over and kissed him, lingeringly, on his forehead.

19

In life, she had never believed in ghosts. Had been quite dismissive of them and anything connected with the afterlife or 'beyond', to be honest.

However, a couple of days after she had died (and to my utter amazement), she appeared to me, as if trying to give me comfort and solace. In the kitchen, in the early evening – twilight time – in the semi-darkness and out of the corner of my eye I thought I caught the briefest of movements. I glanced up and there she was, a mere few feet away. Her hair was as it had been all those years ago: luxuriant and full and with those reddish flecks. She was in her green paisley dress, and the colours of both her hair and the dress put me in mind of early autumn. She was smiling, beaming at me; her eyes alive and glistening as they had been when I first knew her. She did not speak, but seemed to be silently reassuring me. I stared at her and blew a slow, long kiss. Slowly, she raised the fingers of her right hand to her lips and returned the gesture. Then, after a few all-too-short moments, she faded before my eyes and vanished in a pinpoint of light at about the height of her head.

I stood rooted to the spot, dumbfounded, almost unbelieving, yet grateful. I hoped that it would happen again but, thus far, it hasn't. It's been eight months now. Perhaps it takes too much energy on their part to come back through the ether? Or is it all some kind of mirage, maybe? Or merely a fervent and delusional wish on my part to see her again for one more time? But somewhere, however far away, I was certain that she was around, and I took comfort and consolation from that.

Then I remembered – could almost feel again, as I closed my eyes and rocked gently on my heels in the encroaching darkness – how I used to stand behind her at the cooker and put my arms around her breasts, while kissing the nape of her neck which was dotted with skin tags. In that small, fuggy kitchen, yes, with the sauna-like steam rising from the saucepans and obliterating the window that looked out onto the garden; the garden and the plants to which she had devoted herself and which she tended daily.

Those times have irrevocably gone, yet they echo…they echo… echo down the days and nights…those long nights…

20

In the following weeks, he had a recurrent dream. She was straddling him, pinning him fiercely to the grass on that hot summer's day up on the hills. She wasn't making love to him, but slapping his face in time to the various accusations that she was making. The sun was directly overhead, almost blinding him, and his right cheek stung and she just wouldn't shut up, wouldn't let it go, and she felt heavy on his chest, even though she was fairly petite and... Oh, for Christ's sake! I can't bloody breathe and I can't take much more of this...

21

They never saw each other again. But just that once, fleetingly, years later, she thought that she had glimpsed him.

She had boarded a train at Manchester Piccadilly to head south, and had settled into her seat. Three minutes until the train departed. She unfolded her paper, but not before she randomly glanced across at the adjacent carriage. To her astonishment, there he was in the window seat almost opposite her, head down, intent on looking at something on his laptop. He didn't look up. The hair, the profile and the colouring were identical, but had she somehow imagined it? Perhaps, however weirdly (and despite her inner stern denials), she had wanted it to be him?

She would never know, for at that moment her train began to draw out of the station, sliding away smoothly from the platform, almost apologetically and regretfully, or so it seemed to her. Angrily, she flicked over a page of her paper, trying to erase thoughts of him, but failed.

22

He was dreaming the same dream. He had dozed off after lunch in his chair by the fire. He slowly came to amid the unending clamour of shellfire. And there, full on in his line of vision, was the face of his mate Bill, gaunt and haunted-looking. He appeared to be shouting, but no words escaped his lips. He seemed, judging by his unsettled demeanour and the evident terror in his eyes, to want to relay an urgent message. But whatever it was, that message could not be uttered. Then, moments later, Bill's face vanished, as if it had been wiped from the godawful face of the earth. He stared across the endless deep mud and bodies to no man's land. The dimming twilit sky was already becoming an eerie navy blue, while the gunfire was gradually becoming sparser, more intermittent and echoey. Eventually, much to his relief, it petered out altogether. He thought that he heard a soldier cry out, but couldn't see him.

His wife had taken the bus into town to do some shopping for their tea, and wouldn't be back for some while. He hoped that she'd buy some lean lamb chops. A bit later, he would pick some mint and rosemary from their garden, but not just yet. Mint for the sauce and the potatoes, yes, and a handful of rosemary sprigs for the lamb. He might pick a cabbage, too. A tasty meal, all in all.

Tears welled up yet again and he dried his eyes with his frayed right-hand shirt cuff. With a shaking hand he lit a cigarette, inhaled gratefully, exhaled through his nose (a slow double jet of smoke), and listened to the heavy seconds tick by from the oak clock on the mantelpiece. Sometimes it was all he could do not to hurl that bloody clock into the garden; smash it to smithereens against the drystone wall. Anything to stop that remorseless, infernal ticking that never left his head, moment on endless moment, round and around and around, unceasingly…

23

He was on a train, northbound from Manchester. Opening up his laptop, he glanced over to the adjacent train and thought, for a mere split second, that he saw her face, but dismissed the thought instantly, deciding that he was just being sentimental and must have imagined it. She was opening a newspaper. He kept his head down and started to answer his emails.

It had been years ago, anyway, and he was now married with two children: one of each sex. Logically, he supposed that he was a lucky man, but he rarely felt it. Every year, his wife and kids seemed to cost him a small fortune, and increasingly he felt that there was no escape from his hermetic, humdrum existence. He wouldn't call it a life. Yet, he reasoned, there were childless couples who would give their eye teeth for children such as his: caring, polite and generally easy-going; in virtually all ways a credit to their parents. It was a conundrum, that was for sure. What was equally certain was that there were never any easy answers. Of any kind, ever.

He sighed loudly, blew out his cheeks, and began to address the next email which required an urgent response. A girl with a trolley trundled past, and he ordered a coffee.

24

After eight years, he was released from HMP Styal and there she was outside the gate, waiting for him, as faithful and devoted as ever, and smiling a welcome, bless her. God, he was a lucky man. Many wives wouldn't have stood for that: the sheer disgrace of it. She drove him back to Aberdaron, stopping off for lunch en route. It was a rarity for them to eat anywhere but in their own hotel.

He had to readjust all over again to the once-familiar life of the hotelier, and it would take time: possibly several months, if not more. In the village, opinion of him was sharply divided. Some people clapped him on the back and were evidently delighted to see him; while others crossed the road to avoid him, which wasn't easy to face, day in, day out, in such a small place. People glanced at him and whispered behind their hands. At least the local vicar, though an austere, unsmiling man of few words, was supportive; also of their cause and the language.

When the bomb had detonated in the late evening, it had ripped apart a couple of buildings, but caused no injuries or fatalities. Yet, they had all felt entirely justified in their course of action, and it was the gesture that counted. Like a latter-day Saunders Lewis and his pals, yes. He and three other members of the Men of Glyndŵr had been arrested within the week. Some treacherous bastard had spilled the beans. He would have loved to know who and, given half a chance, rearrange their face for them…

25

His strength was slowly ebbing away and his wife had phoned their son to come and say goodbye and make peace with his dying father. All the father wished for now was to be reunited with his parents, their dead daughter, and Bill.

The train journey from Cornwall was slow and tedious, giving the son much time to concentrate his thoughts on the father who had never been close to him; had always seemed preoccupied, stiff and distant. After several hours and a change at Bristol Temple Meads, the train arrived, twenty minutes late, in Harrogate and he took a taxi to the small cottage in the hills, about five miles away. As he crossed the threshold, he and his mother just held each other silently, not speaking.

After a cup of tea, the son steeled himself to climb the stairs, turn the worn brass knob of the bedroom door, stoop to enter, and be given the strength to make peace with his father. Odd that, at such a time as this, he should be wishing for strength for himself, rather than for his rapidly ailing father. The room smelt musty and he went over to open the window before gently greeting his father. He sat down on one side of the bed, his face close to his father's hollow, yellowed face on the dishevelled couple of thin pillows. The old man stirred slightly and winced. His son reached for his bony, withered hand and held it, but not too tightly.

'Dad. It's me.'

A faint, flickering smile as he attempted to lift himself up on the pillows to face his son, whom he had not seen since the previous Christmas, almost a year ago.

'No need to sit up, Dad. You're fine as you are.'

'I'm not bloody fine, I'm dying.' A few coughs and splutters, but still defiant.

'Yes, I know. That's why I've come.'

Then the father looked straight into his son's eyes with a surprisingly fierce light. 'I'm...sorry, son. I owe you an...an apology. All these years and I... I never showed you, never told you that I was proud of you.'

'You had problems of your own, Dad. Too many problems.' He looked away and out of the small window across the patchwork of brilliant, verdant fields, and then back to his father.

'Can you forgive me? Can you?' An urgent pleading tone now in the thin, wheezing voice.

The son's face lowered for a moment and paused. 'Of course, Dad.' He swallowed hard. Suddenly his throat was terribly dry, despite the recent cup of tea. 'Yes, I forgive you.'

His father seemed to relax.

The son let go his hand. 'Just going to the loo, Dad,' he said, and walked the short distance to the bathroom. Amid the silence, the sound of his peeing and the flush seemed noisier than ever; an unwelcome intrusion.

He returned to the bedside. The bunch of lavender stems that his mother had picked, then tied together and placed carefully on her husband's bedside table fragranced the room and lessened the smell of illness. His father had closed his eyes and looked peaceful; his head turned away to the right. It took the son a few moments to realise that he had slipped away. At the moment of his death, two good things had happened: the clock in his head had stopped ticking and the gunfire had ceased.

As the son made his way down the stairs, his mother was coming up. She looked at his face and knew immediately. 'He's out of his pain now,' she said.

'Let's hope that he's at peace,' he said, frowning.

She nodded, turned, and went back to refill the kettle on the stove. It was a familiar gesture in the middle of an unfamiliar scenario, and at that precise moment it was the only thing she could think of to do.

A month later, three days after his funeral, she and her sister were sorting out his things. In the back right-hand corner of his sock and underwear drawer was a small, dilapidated, navy-blue box. She opened it carefully to find three medals from the First World War. They were a little tarnished, but not too bad, given that that war had ended forty years ago. Typically, he had never mentioned them; not even once. The ribbons were intact and, for a long moment, she held each of them proudly in turn between her hands, before returning them, with a kiss, to the worn box.

26

He gave it a year, but in his long enforced absence she had taken over the hotel on the beachfront, and kept the business afloat. What else could she have done, given the situation? Mostly, it was the locals wanting their regular pint and the occasional meal out, but in the summer it was busy with the tourist trade from the Midlands, Merseyside and the Wirral; pretty much non-stop from mid-May until mid-September. More often than not, he felt like an unwanted guest in his own home, though he tried to keep cheerful and busy, flushing out the pipes and tending to the barrels while she did the ordering in of both drink and food. The ignominy of it, however, was hard to bear.

Before going to bed, they often looked over to the island with their binoculars, but never again did they see the saints and the angels ascending slowly to heaven from within the cloud. The cloud of knowing – or, more likely, he felt, of unknowing.

It had been very quiet all that evening, with barely a soul in either bar. Just before closing time, he said he was going out for a walk; wanted to get some air and be by himself to think. He had been thinking a lot recently. He decided not to take the dog, although she wagged her tail in anticipation of a late-night walk, looking up at him hopefully with those bright, devoted eyes. Brighter and more loving, he had to admit, than his wife's eyes…

He quietly closed the back door and started to walk purposefully from the beach at Aberdaron along to Whistling Sands. In keeping with that name, the wind was rising steadily, moaning and keening like a banshee. He kept walking, head down, hoping that no one was out on that fierce, treacherous sea. The wind began to howl around him and the rain to gust in horizontally from the sea. He stopped, lowered the soaking hood of his anorak, glanced back towards Aberdaron for a few seconds and, timing it to perfection (as he had been taught, back in the day), fired a single shot into his right temple.

The previous night's storm had blown itself out and the sun was shining brightly. Just after 8am, his corpse was discovered by a couple exercising their dog.

A couple of hours later, there was a knock on the door of the hotel. A stony-faced policeman stood there, twisting his helmet in his hands awkwardly, waiting to give the widow the bad news.

27

And here comes jolly Uncle Jack Death, wishing to hug us, constrict us, boa-like, into submission. But he won't kill us swiftly, oh no. No, he'll take his time all right; play with us, toy with us; a glint and a hint in the fading, failing sunlight off his scythe. Smiling slowly, stroking his moustache, while the whole time he's taking the piss. 'A touch of cancer? Neither here nor there really – nothing too drastic or upfront, old boy. Not yet. No, that will all come later with the chemo and the drips, the boredom, fatigue and fear, but not necessarily in that order. Stretching it all out? Oh yes indeed, old fruit. We've got months to go yet. Best to have something in reserve, eh, old bean?' Bastard Uncle Jack Death, with his reassuring, patrician voice. 'My dear chap, we've all got to go at some point, don't you know?' Sounding and looking like some upper-class twat straight out of a P. G. Wodehouse novel, in his plus fours, two-tone shoes, and razor-sharp central parting in his slicked-down, Brylcreemed hair...

Shadows...shadows on scans...longer shadows...the shadows of endless, moonlit nights in the hospital...fading, receding voices... the masked look of the doctor's face behind his mask...light fading...drifting...

Uncle Death is tightening his embrace on me now. I can feel his breath on my face…hear insinuating whispers in my ear, but gently, so gently…sounds of running water…am I drowning? Am I? Am I?

I am

I am no longer

No longer me

Where am I?

What am I?

Ah!

He who hath reached the yon and nigh of things,
So all are ended, quenched and are no more,
Calm man, and in attachment's end released,
Oblation-worthy is the Man-thus-come!
(Buddha)

Acknowledgements

With sincere thanks to the SilverWood team for designing and publishing my books, and to you, my readers.

Printed in Great Britain
by Amazon

37150499R00108